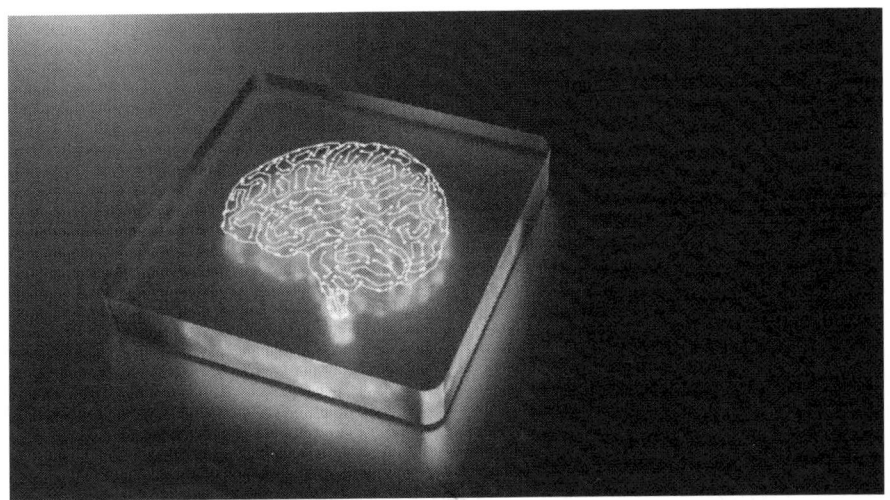

First Published in paperback in 2020

Copyright © 2020 Jim Kemp

Jim Kemp has asserted his right to be identified as the author of this work in accordance with the Copyright, Designs and Patents Act 1988

ISBN 9798683488772

All rights reserved. No part of this publication may be reproduced, stored in a retrieval system or transmitted in any form or by any means, electronic, mechanical, photocopying, recording or otherwise, without the prior permission of the author.

Names, characters, companies and events within the story are either the products of the author's imagination or used in a fictitious manner. Any resemblance to actual persons; living or dead, companies or events is purely coincidental. Any opinions expressed within the context of the story do not represent those of the author.

Jim Kemp

THE DREAM WATCHER

Never Lose Track of Your Dreams

A special thank you to my editorial team:

John & Carol Kemp

(Otherwise known as my dad and mum)

I appreciate the help and support you have always given me

I'll see you in my dreams
And then I'll hold you in my dreams
Someone took you right out of my arms
Still I feel the thrill of your charms

Lips that once were mine
Tender eyes that shine
They will light my way tonight
I'll see you in my dreams...

Songwriters: Gus Kahn / Isham Jones
I'll See You in My Dreams lyrics © Sony/ATV Music Publishing LLC,
Warner Chappell Music, Inc

CHAPTER 1

THE YEAR 2042...

*'Come with me and you'll be
In a world of your imagination
Take a look and you'll see
Into your imagination
You'll begin with a spin
Travelling in the world of your creation
What you'll see will defy your explanation'*...

The music played from the speakers of the built-in TV set in one of the kitchen cupboards as Jared made a coffee; his eyes fixed to the Dreamex advert as it ran its course; trying to adjust his tie in between taking bites from his toast and creating a metallic backing-track from his over-stirring throughout. He was proud to work for the company who were now ratcheting up their marketing campaign for the Dream Watcher; the world's first piece of tech that could not only interpret people's dreams but record them and enable playback on any device.

The release date was just prior to Christmas, now only eight months away but orders had already gone through the roof in spite of its astronomical price-tag.

Despite other inventions having already changed the face of society in so many ways over the previous two decades and huge strides having been made in transportation, renewable energy, health and space exploration; the Dream Watcher was like nothing else; and Dreamex knew they were onto a winner, following almost ten years of research and development.

The ability to record and replay dreams had always been seen as one of life's impossibilities; a feat only achievable, ironically, in the daydreams of those with a vivid imagination.

Up until that point, the understanding of dreams was the exclusive province of dream analysts, generic self-help literature and oneirology, the study of dreams, which was concerned with the related processes of the brain's functionality.

Everyone dreamt but not everyone could remember them after waking; and even for those who could; they would soon forget and lose the thread. Forgetting dreams was normal as memories of them would quickly fade. With the new tech, people would have the ability to own a copy of every single one of their dreams; a back-catalogue of their own creations and be able to replay them at their own leisure, like choosing to watch a film or TV box set.

Jared had been part of Dreamex since the development phase of the project; his anxiety problems having made him a perfect fit for the company's search for 'Dreamers'. He had a continually overactive imagination, causing him to experience much greater unconscious brain activity during sleep than the average person, and therefore an invaluable source of dream material.

Today was going to be a crucial day for Jared. He had something he needed to do and it was imperative he managed to pull it off. It represented by far the biggest violation of company policy; certain to get him fired if caught, although there could be much worse repercussions for him as a result. That's why he'd planned it out meticulously. His own and other peoples' futures depended on it and he was aware of its significance.

Having let Sprocket, his West Highland Terrier, in from the back, he'd already decanted some biscuits into his bowl and made sure to top up the water next to it, patting him on the head as he guzzled them down, not stopping to take a breath.

'You're going to be late Jared, and I think I'd wear a coat if I were you; it's only ten degrees Celsius out there,' came the lucid voice from a youthful Cindy Crawford, who's face now appeared on the same TV-unit, Jared having selected her as his personal home-hub assistant, which had automatically paused the current VT briefly to advise him. Quickly peering over at the clock on the wall, he sipped another mouthful of hot coffee and picked up the remaining piece of toast, before rushing to the front door and grabbing his jacket from the rack in the hallway. He ensured he had his Dream Watcher in his bag, from which he'd wiped the memory the previous night, after transferring the data.

'Don't mention it,' Cindy hollered rolling her eyes, the system detecting that Jared had left the house without any response and something that it had been well used to by now.

Jared got into his car; an Illusion 500; a small battery-powered vehicle that seated four, the front seats which could rotate to face the rear passengers; no centre console as gear sticks and handbrakes had been obsolete for years, the drive-train all taken care of automatically from new onboard computer technology and the driver only needing to depress the accelerator and direct the car onto the nearest shuttle-lane.

Most roads were now lined with sensors that communicated back and forth with each individual vehicle and kept traffic moving at the same speed, the driver only requiring to choose when they wanted to exit to their final destination. In fact, the driver didn't even have to do that if they told their onboard computer where they wanted to travel to before setting off, the vehicle's tracking system planning the route and feeding the information via the shuttle-lane sensors and allowing the driver to sit back, prepare for a business meeting or even finish their breakfast.

It was seldom that companies arranged for physical meetings anymore; the lockdown period during COVID-19 throughout 2020 and 2021 having highlighted the success of home-working and shifted the shape of businesses in general. This was especially true for those in the tertiary or service sectors, which now made up 62% of the UK's gross domestic product, a decrease on levels from decades before following the development of new battery technology that arose from chemistry labs at Lancaster University, and which were now seen as the gold standard that all countries around the world who hadn't already, wanted to adopt.

The manufacturing of the batteries had rocketed, companies taking over old power stations, refineries and steel industrial sites in the North of England, having once been the building blocks and major employers that led to the country's economic rise at the beginning and towards the middle of the 20th Century.

The advance in battery technology had not only created a cleaner world but the power and longevity of the new battery cells had meant they were the most practical and cheapest form of power, used extensively in transportation; in cars, buses and even lorries; haulage firms saving millions in fuel overheads in the long-term after initial outlays on new fleets of vehicles. The battery could not only deliver the same power from one-quarter of the size of previous cells but meant charging was made pretty much redundant; a 4-PAK able to kinetically charge the three dormant batteries whilst running on the current one and therefore limits on journey ranges a thing of the past.

As fossil fuels were depleting and had been squeezed out in favour of new technology, then the giant petrochemical companies had redirected their focus in order to remain relevant; not only embracing efficient batteries but developing on existing renewable energy through advanced solar cells. However, the real breakthrough had come from harnessing the colossal might of lightning; these household names having devised huge factories known as Eco-Rods in countries with relatively low lightning-activity that could mimic the necessary weather conditions to create small-scale strikes and then channel its energy through advanced electrostatic charging stations housing thousands if not millions of 4-PAK batteries destined for the global market.

Many larger scale models of the Eco-Rod had initially been set up in the late 2020's/ early 2030's on the African continent; cheaper to build and to run and home to six of the world's top ten sites for lightning strikes, located along the Mitumba Mountains in Eastern Congo and 1000 miles north-east on the shores of Lake Victoria in Kampala, Uganda, which experienced 242 days of thunderstorms per year on average, more than any other country in the world.

Although Boeing and Airbus had invested heavily in engine manufacturing companies to implement the same battery technology to power their aircraft; experimenting with lining hundreds of cells within the voids in the wings which were previously the aircraft's fuel tanks; airline travel had been dwindling. People choosing staycations over holidaying abroad and the rise in global video-conferencing as a result of the Coronavirus lockdown had meant the demand just wasn't there anymore; a shift in the way society operated, and those airlines lucky enough to survive the months of forced grounding were never able to recapture the same levels of business thereafter.

COVID-19 had been a fatal bird-strike through the aviation industry's turbine. Interestingly, Concorde's crash in 2000 had, in effect, brought an end to supersonic travel, albeit continuing to fly until 2003; airlines having been more interested in carrying increased numbers of passengers subsonic than relatively few at twice the speed of sound. It had indeed been a rather strange phenomenon for those having lived through 'Speedbird's' 27-year passenger service; to reflect that nobody since had been able to travel as quickly between two points on the globe, seemingly a retreat, instead of an advance, in aviation technology, and which many would never have expected.

CHAPTER 2

Although the reduction in air travel; there had been a rise in the now popular pleasure trips into space; no longer just for the sole enjoyment of the rich given it was comparable to the price of a family holiday. Although only lasting a few hours, it was certainly something that lived up to its billing; an 'out of this world' experience, and apart from the privateers trying to break into the market, some of the airlines had invested hugely too, realising the (gravitational) pull of such an iconic attraction.

Meanwhile, at the business end of spaceflight and exploration, there had been a cold war of sorts; several billionaires vying to become the first to send a manned mission to Mars; the race having started by SpaceX and its newly designed reusable rocket propulsion system that could land remotely on a droid ship in the middle of the Atlantic Ocean; a spectacle that looked like something only ever seen in movies or on Gerry Anderson's 'Thunderbirds'.

Nobody had a claim to the Red Planet and it was unsurprising to many when they learnt that the Russians and Chinese were hot on the coattails of Elon Musk and his space quest. He'd established SpaceX and bankrolled the company, with initial test flights to the International Space Station in 2020 and 2021, before missions to Mars began in the early 2030s. It was the second such mission which proved a success (after losing contact with the initial spacecraft after 96 days into its journey); the unmanned drone rocket having landed a capsule with equipment and life-support systems for a future crew to locate and utilise after the extensive planning and necessary science had been invented.

The largest worldwide audience ever recorded for a live event gathered around their holographic TVs to witness the launch of the Shuttle Enterprise from Cape Kennedy in June 2040; the first ever manned spaceflight that would attempt to reach the Red Planet. The build up to the event had been colossal and had touched everyone's imagination. Given the logistics involved; the six crew were still seven months out from reaching its destination along its scheduled 889-day journey. Having agreed that they would conserve fuel and not rush the mission, they forwent using full afterburners but would still be travelling at a relative speed of 5,764mph, over seven times the speed of sound, although there was no sound in deep space. Their velocity would help to reduce travel time by 19% over the baseline for the 123-million-mile journey, a distance which was 12% under the average distance between the two planets given their differing orbital paths around the sun.

Developments in rocket fuel technology had meant that the Enterprise and its earlier iterations had not had to carry such an excessive amount of fuel, which had previously been suggested; figures of approximately four tonnes instead of seven per one-tonne-payload having been the revised calculation in order for it to successfully orbit with Mars on arrival. The maths had been proven correct; the success of Shuttle New Hope testament to that.

If everything went according to plan, then the late Neil Armstrong's 41-year-old granddaughter, Piper Van Wagenen, would be the first to set foot on the Red Planet on 11th November 2042, 73 years 3 months and 24 days after he and Apollo 11 landed on the moon.

The biggest reason for the move away from air travel in general had been due to pollution; the reduction in CO_2 emissions thanks to the empty skies during the COVID crisis; a stark reminder of what the majority had simply accepted as the norm before. Many governments had capitulated to public pressure on cleaner modes of transport moving forwards following sustained protests, and with Greta Thunberg, now in her late thirties, having continued to spearhead the call for adopting new systems in order to help reduce pollution's effect on climate change. The push for greener travel had prompted a new think-tank on alternatives and it was then that the next generation of electric vehicles took-off, although not literally; not flying cars; the general consensus that it still remained an impractical concept; too risky and fraught with problems; driverless cars and the shuttle-lane network springing up instead, and other modes to be kept safely on terra firma for now.

This was especially true on shorter intercontinental routes, with the development of the new Euro-Tube on mainland Europe; a 4-metre diameter overground pipe network which housed passenger pods that could be jettisoned along at hypersonic speed using vacuum technology, and which had utilised the existing oil-pipeline infrastructure of the petrochemical industry as the basis for testing and route selection; connecting major cities within Europe and adding more to service the popular holiday destinations to the south. Although several private companies in Denmark, Switzerland and France had been working separately on similar concepts; a joint treaty, following the collaboration of the EU35 countries, had chosen the most practicable version in order to ensure universality across all affected member states.

The idea had stemmed from the James Bond film, The Living Daylights; although only a one-man bob type set-up had been showcased. In order to be a realistic alternative to train travel and to be economically viable, it was necessary to increase the pipeline's girth to take more passengers, the billions having already been spent on the incomplete HS2 high-speed rail link infrastructure in the UK having not been a complete waste, given it could be adapted to an extension of the new mode of transportation in the future.

Having rejoined the EU, the UK still had a problem though. Its position away from the mainland meant that in order to be connected up to the Euro-Tube on the continent, it would either need to disband with The Chunnel Eurostar train service and reconfigure the existing infrastructure to accommodate the new passenger pods, or build a further 30-mile tunnel under the English Channel.

It wasn't just transportation that had evolved as a result of the Coronavirus pandemic. The crisis, despite directly and indirectly killing millions of people around the world prior to the distribution of an effective vaccine, and for all the suffering as a result, had served as a global pause button. People had no real option but to stop and take stock of their own and others' lives; the vast majority sharing a real unity for the first time, now placed in exactly the same situation as them.

Black Lives Matter campaigning had taken off on a truly and necessary global scale following the murder of George Floyd; coinciding with when many countries were slowly reducing lockdown measures following first waves. The movement to end centuries of systemic and institutionalised racism in the global community had been by far the biggest single positive to come out of it. It was fortuitous in some ways that so many from all walks of life were able to actively take part in continual demonstrations, given the conditions of work being placed on hold and people riding it out at home under the reduced freedom they'd bought into to try to mitigate the spread of the virus.

Two decades later, there was now a noticeable change in society across the board; people of all ethnicities given the same opportunities in education and employment despite social standings and almost everyone had reached the same page. There were still those that remained bigoted in their views and the odd demonstration cropping up, but thankfully they were a lot fewer and less frequent than had been anticipated, and that had gone on for too long before.

Chapter 3

Jared usually spent his 20-minute commute checking the car's drop-down 14-inch entertainment display; his mobile automatically cast onto it and able to use the touch screen controls as though using a giant version of his own phone. There was a message from Cindy wishing him a good day at work and an update on what groceries and other household supplies he was running low on; sensors in his kitchen cupboards, fridge and freezer able to read bar codes and expiry dates and keep him informed of what he needed to use first; automatically updating his shopping-list-app and placing an order with the supermarket depot for delivery as per his previously selected preference each week.

Thirty-six percent of the world's population were now self-certified as vegan, plant-based meat-substitutes so like the real thing that it left many realising that changing their diet was no longer a difficult decision to make.

Almost everything was fully automated nowadays and even plugs were a thing of the past, new tech coming with long-lasting rechargeable batteries or included remote-charging hardware, a small aerial which could connect wirelessly to the home-loop, an electric field that sat inside the walls of the house and that powered the peripheral equipment when switched on. Jared had always been surprised how and why plugs had lasted so long, although realised they must have been a cheap and practical option for tech companies to use when selling electronic devices.

The Dream Watcher used wireless technology and Jared liked that; he hated wires and remembered how his old cinema room had annoyed him, yards and yards of cable connected up to his entertainment cabinet akin to a Pink Floyd concert.

But above all inventions that had become the norm of the future, Jared's personal favourite was the new plastic technology within cling-film; no longer his most frustrating daily gripe when trying to spool it off the roll without it sticking to itself at every possible stage, and which had made the task almost impossible. New cling-film gave you at least two minutes after tearing off before it automatically pulled tight around the object you were covering; a real breakthrough as far as he was concerned.

Jared had always been enthusiastic heading into work, until very recently. Dreamex would soon be providing him with a final version of the Dream Watcher to take home, prior to its general release later in the year; earlier glitches having been successfully ironed out, or so the powers that be would have everyone believe. The truth was, had he not worked for Dreamex, then he'd never have been able to afford one, the gadget far too expensive and only a consideration for the wealthy. Still, he would be a pioneer; after spending years helping to provide data and contribute to the project, it would soon be D-Day and a chance for him to see the finished product, all shiny and new and packaged neatly in its aluminium presentation case.

After exiting the shuttle-lane and steering the final few hundred yards, Jared could see the familiar and futuristic looking Dreamex Corporation building towering above the other nearby companies, its silver window-surrounds glistening. A large portion of the glass panes to the front were tinted; an automatic reaction to the direct sunlight, helping to shade office workers as well as being part of the intelligent system to control and regulate internal temperature. This was now the norm for new builds and homeowners who were keen to switch over to the new technology.

    Parking up in his usual space, Jared got out of his car; no key required given it could detect exactly who he was from biometric scanners built into the top of the doors and handles. He then walked briskly to the entrance steps, noting he only had three minutes to get in and up to the top floor where he was joining the other 'Dreamers' for a meeting with the CEO, Alexander Van Tam.

CHAPTER 4

5 Years Earlier....

Jared Blake was 38 years old; single, recently unemployed and lived on his own. Having been made redundant from his job at the bank after 14 years, this was the first real time he'd had to look for work since leaving university, and he was finding it more difficult than he'd expected. His previous experience and degree in mathematical studies didn't seem to count for too much in the real world; AI technology having created a surplus of low to mid-skilled workers through the rise of intelligent robotics, the better paid jobs now highly sought after and the competition increased enormously as a result.

His plight in gaining employment had also come at a time when legislation, first brought out by a new Labour government in 2025; effectively made it compulsory for all businesses, that employed more than 50 staff, to make their recruitment processes more robust and transparent; a special branch of the Department for Work and Pensions set up to carry out spot checks to ensure affected companies were embracing meritocracy and the mantra of equal opportunities for all.

Previous initiatives on diversity and inclusion had been bandied about liberally on social media platforms and via government taskforces for the previous decade but with little progress made. In fact many companies had simply treated it as a box-ticking exercise; propelling new ethnic minority staff across their website and media channels from day one in a bid to create public appeal and make them appear an inclusive company. Jared, however, knew it just wasn't the case, having experienced the sham first-hand; those same staff not given the same levels of support or scope for career progression by peers or senior management. After realising they didn't have the backing or tools to mount a realistic challenge to their situation; many had no other choice but to walk away after only a matter of weeks.

Jared didn't really know what he wanted to do with his life at that stage; still hopeful he'd meet the right girl and settle down with a family of his own; but at this juncture, a stable income was the priority and something which would be the foundation of his other aspirations. Then one day, his luck changed; he received a call from his best mate Troy, who he'd known since playschool and was genuinely concerned about his friend.

'I've just seen a job advertised in Chester and I think it'd be perfect for you; you've got to apply!' Troy announced, his face having appeared on the left-hand-side of the TV-screen in Jared's lounge, the other half continuing to show the sports news channel he was watching, although at a reduced volume.

'Aye aye fellameladdo…perfect hey? What's it about?'

'Well you know you're always remembering your dreams and telling us about them when we all meet up? Well there's a company called Dreamex who are looking to recruit participants to assist them with their study into dreams and are looking for people just like you…it's decent pay too.'

'So, let them carry out research on me, you mean?' Jared replied laughing at the concept.

'Says they're carrying out 'auditions' next week, so why not go check it out? Easy money if you ask me.'

'Okay, well I haven't exactly got people banging my door down to offer me a job...may just do that...have you got the details?'

'Just check out Dreamex on The Cloud and it'll all be there.'

'Nice one bud...I'll have a look now.'

After saying their goodbyes, Jared spoke to the home-hub to bring up the Dreamex site on the TV; Cindy confirming his command and he was now looking at the company's bio. He'd never heard of them before but the whole dream study had whetted his appetite and he was certainly interested to find out more.

Navigating his way through their job adverts, he found the one that Troy had mentioned and at £35 an hour, it seemed like a very good offer indeed. 'Play video,' Jared exclaimed and with that the CEO of Dreamex appeared on screen.

'Hello and thank you for showing an interest in a future role with us here at Dreamex. I'm Alexander Van Tam, the CEO and I'm here to explain what we're looking for. Perhaps you can help us. I set up the company five years ago; the goal to better understand the way in which our brains work, how they store memories and more importantly how this memory is utilised during the process of dreaming. In order to carry out qualitative research; there's one thing missing though...'Dreamers'...

If you are prone to frequent dreaming or better still you're the type to remember them, then please come along to one of our open days for an audition...yes, it's an audition not a job interview so no need to gen-up on techniques or worry about what to wear; we're only interested in your brain activity; that's it. If you think you have an overactive brain or a history of vivid dreaming, then come along... and if we agree with you, then you'll be given the opportunity to join a great company and one I promise will not only look after you but enable you to become an integral member of the team. Just submit your details using the online video registration portal and leave the rest to us. Thank you for listening to me and who knows; your dreams may come true at Dreamex.'

    Jared scrunched his face up on hearing the CEO's cheesy line to end on but it hadn't put him off in the slightest; now keener than before to audition. After leaving his details as requested, Jared now checked out Dreamex's location, calling up the live satellite feed via the home-assistant and able to zoom in and around their headquarters, approximately 18 miles from where he lived and just over a twenty-minute commute via the local shuttle-lanes. Jared was excited and sent Troy a short message to thank him and to say he'd signed-up.

Chapter 5

The day of the audition had arrived; the last week had seemed to have gone slower than usual as Jared just wanted to know if his brain activity would be sufficient to get him a job. He knew they were looking for around 25-30 Dreamers in total but given the prerequisite to audition was only having a brain and little else, then he knew there'd be a large contingent in exactly the same boat as he; also seeing pound signs for very little effort. In order to try to excel during whatever tests they would be carrying out; Jared had gone big with the cheese in his diet, having eaten a 4-cheese pizza for dinner and now cheese on toast for breakfast. He'd seen the results for himself and knew it wasn't an old wives' tale; he had to give himself every possible chance for success.

Despite what Van Tam had said; Jared had still wanted to make an effort with his appearance, his two-tone suit pressed and his hair remodelled using the now commonplace Hairkutz 3000, an old-fashioned looking hair-dryer-heater that sat like an oversized helmet on the user, but whose hidden technology could cut, shave, colour, dry and style anybody's hair; only having to add the colour dye or product before selecting an option. It was possibly 'the best gadget' that had ever been invented in Jared's mind, the process dramatically reducing the time taken to have his hair cut and styled by a hairdresser.

Hairdressing was still big business despite the invention, a great number still preferring the interaction of a human. The rise of the HairKutz 3000 had been the result of the COVID crisis, the vast majority of people who couldn't have their hair cut for months and coming out of lockdown looking like

Shaggy from Scooby Doo; or having the ignominy of having a botched effort that their nearest and dearest had attempted, which had seemed like a good idea at the time.

Jared couldn't help feeling it was like being back in his old routine when working at the bank; having to get up earlier, shower and prepare for a day away from his home, having spent the last seven months mostly lounging in his pyjamas as he'd had no real reason to go out. Taking a shower nowadays gave him slight cause for concern though, since having the new one fitted a couple of years earlier.

The Home Medi-Cube, which could be a stand-alone unit in someone's bedroom or built into a shower cubicle, had sensors in its walls which scanned the individual; taking just a couple of minutes to record weight, height, body mass index, heart rate, temperature and detect any changes to the skin; even checking for potential heart disease. Connected wirelessly to the home-assistant, Cindy would then verbally confirm if Jared had passed his daily MOT or would automatically contact his doctor if it discovered anything serious that required a follow-up.

Arriving at Dreamex Corporation's new headquarters just outside Chester in good time for his audition, Jared got a very good feeling they meant business; the 5-storey building glistening in the mid-morning sunshine and looking in every way part of a science-led company of the future.

A communication had been sent out to all would-be 'Dreamers', including Jared, laying out the schedule for the day; those lucky enough to be selected for roles within the company asked to remain in situ for the afternoon sessions; those not having made the grade having to leave at noon on receipt of their results.

After congregating outside on the impressive entrance steps, there was then a sudden advance; a few of the more confident types spearheading the group, a throng of 100 or so nervous individuals following behind and into the vast and somewhat sparse reception area. There was, however, no reception desk; nor it appeared anybody to greet them.

There were groups of people from seemingly every demographic; young, old, black, white, mixed-race, physically-disabled and even the rare sight of a blind person, successful medical procedures having been in place for many years to rectify the condition through advanced ocular transplants, although evident that there were still some waiting to benefit from it. Jared had been surprised to see a blind person come to the audition; the concept of someone who couldn't see having dreams was something that seemed rather strange.

As the noise began to crescendo following tentative polite conversation; there was suddenly a universal silence. Everyone was being cast into darkness as a wave of opaqueness shimmied across the vast glass panels that made up the front facade, shutting out the light little by little; a few having noticed the huge screen that was now descending simultaneously from the ceiling above.

It was almost pitch-black and with that there was an explosion of colour, the candidates witnessing a stunning presentation showcasing Dreamex's arrival into the pantheon of science and technology, and their enthusiasm and confidence was a sight to behold. The blind person did not lose out completely, having received a special earpiece by post from the company which automatically sent a real-time description of what the others and Jared could see. After the company's promises and cultural aspirations had been displayed throughout the light show, there was a momentary black-out. An excitable tension palpable as the room remained in silence. Then, a face everyone recognised appeared on the screen; it was Alexander Van Tam and he had a few words for those who had come along.

'Good morning and welcome to Dreamex...It's great to see you all here. As you already know, in order to ascertain if you're the correct fit for our research programme then we'll need to carry out some simple tests whilst under sleep conditions. In order for us to do this and not have to wait for each of you to fall asleep naturally, we'll be carrying out a very safe and common procedure used extensively in medicine; using a barbiturate which will act to anaesthetise you for a maximum of ten minutes and thus allow us enough time to measure your levels of resting brain activity. As you've already signed a consent form and a non-disclosure-agreement, then unless any of you have changed your minds; please step forward so that we can find out which of you will be assisting us with our research into the world of dreams.'

As Van Tam's protracted smile lingered, the screen went blank again and the doors to four large lifts, two on either side of the grand sweeping staircase opened, their lights now encouraging them to climb aboard. The doors closed and all travelled up to the fourth floor in complete synchronicity, everyone exiting and congregating on the expansive hallway overlooking the Cheshire plain without much conversation.

Seconds later, the large group was then surrounded by 12 figures dressed in the same style uniform; a red plastic looking jumpsuit with white chevrons running down one side, from the top of the shoulder, right the way down their trousers to the ankle. They each wore hybrid training shoes which were predominantly red leather with a white welt connecting the uppers to the soles made from next-generation memory foam, able to adjust to the topography of the surface and ensure that the wearer's foot remained perfectly poised with every step.

Although futuristic in appearance, there seemed little in the way of individualism on show; each donned in full face helmets of aluminium silver with an opaque black visor, the wearers' identities remaining a mystery.

'What's happening now?' asked the blind woman, called Rebecca, who stood near to Jared. Jared waited for someone else to respond; his first thought to answer her with 'I know this might sound a tad weird but it appears we've just been joined by the Power Rangers,' his deep sense of intrigue and nervousness at the upcoming tests the only reasons preventing him from laughing out loud at his own observation.

The Dreamex clones then separated the hopefuls into smaller groups; each leading eight or ten of them to a different testing area on the same floor and into a holding room annexed to each of them, where they sat and waited their turn. Calling them out in pairs, they were then led to an adjoining laboratory complete with two dentist chairs and asked to don a sleep mask and headphones, before lying down and making themselves comfortable. A relaxing soundtrack was then piped in whilst also relaying step-by-step updates on the procedure taking place in real time.

Scientists then entered and placed several electrostatic sensors on both of their heads, which were connected remotely to hardware and monitors behind a two-way mirror in an adjoining room. After administering the barbiturates, they left to track the subjects' levels of unconscious brain activity.

It only took a matter of minutes to discern whether the subject was presenting more brain activity than average, especially concerning accessing the parts of the cerebral member that dealt specifically with the storage and utilisation of their short-term memory.

Jared sat waiting his turn, his brain buzzing with activity, as he considered the fact that despite having made it as far as the testing lab, he and everyone else were still in the dark about what Dreamex were actually planning to do with the research data. Perhaps the whole link to dreams was just pretence to enable them to study the brain in more general terms and there was a more sinister reason behind it.

Non-disclosure-agreements and consent forms seemed pretty serious but Jared was reassured by the many others in exactly the same situation as he. He remained upbeat about his impending test and presumed those making it through to the next stages would be provided with a lot more detail, especially as they would be asked to sign a contract with Dreamex.

CHAPTER 6

After the tests had all been completed and everyone was back sitting in the holding rooms, the wait was finally over; a screen housed in the walls displayed the names of those who had passed and who Dreamex wanted to retain. A mix of rejoicing and audible sighing rang out after each had learnt of their fate, the disgruntled majority now filing out towards the lifts and descending down to the main exit flanked by the Power Rangers.

Jared sat very still, staring at his name on the screen and allowed himself a zealous fist pump at successfully making it through to the next stage, when the unlucky ones had departed.

The fourteen selected Dreamers were then escorted to a large auditorium on the top floor and asked to sit on the two front rows nearest the stage. No sooner had they taken their seats when small monitors rose up from the desks in front of them, displaying 'Dreamex Contract' and each applicant asked to select their names from a dropdown list and to follow the on-screen instructions. After reading and swiping through the minutiae; the only thing left for them to do was to sign, confirming their agreement to the terms and conditions and become Dreamex's newest recruits; the screens furling back into the desk recesses and leaving a smooth surface on completion.

Jared had deliberately taken his time to read all of the details, one of the last to put finger to screen and make his contract official. After the last monitor had been safely stowed and before any time for discussions amongst the chosen few, the lights slowly dimmed to darkness and the stage whirred into life. A series of holographic images beamed upwards from the stage-floor creating a crystal clear vision captivating the onlookers. It was finally time for Dreamex to divulge what plans they had for the successful applicants.

The first few minutes were taken up with an introductory piece on how the company was first established and how they had spent the last five years carrying out scientific research on the human brain. They had managed to reboot a human cerebral member through an advanced electrochemical forcefield; the energy substituting the body's own natural processes for maintaining brainwaves and to enable physiological commands.

Jared sat wide-eyed, not really knowing what to think. He was intrigued on the one hand, but left feeling that breaking down and comparing the brain to a piece of hardware was over trivialising its complexities; Dreamex suggesting the average adult brain was akin to a 1000-terabyte hard-drive with enough memory to store the whole works of Shakespeare, Dickens and Tolstoy's War and Peace over 37-million times.

There was then a lesson on the components of the brain; the narrator explaining how it represented the core of the body's nervous system, and the concept that they'd set out to achieve, whilst a large 3D holographic example slowly rotated 10-feet above the stage. It was indeed 'biology for dummies', similar to that of John Hammond's take in Jurassic Park when explaining dinosaur DNA and how they had sourced it from insects preserved in amber to recreate them in test tubes.

They referred to neurons as electrically excitable cells that were capable of both processing and transmitting information via electrochemical signalling, and each one connected up to thousands of others; data passing amongst them through as many as 1,000 trillion synaptic connections, equivalent by some estimates to a computer with a 1-trillion-bit-per-second processor.

Neurogenesis, the process of neurons dividing to create new cells, was commonplace throughout the human body and the reason for growth and ageing throughout our lives. However, unlike the majority of other neurons; those neurons located in the brain were only able to divide to make new cells during foetal development and for a few months after birth. That was apart from the hippocampus, the area of the brain that was in essence the memory, continuously being raided and utilised, never left alone for a second and even operating during our sleep through what we knew as dreaming; like a computer in standby mode, still ticking over underneath a seemingly lifeless and unresponsive exterior.

The complexity of the brain was unquestionable; the reason why, after so much time spent on scientific research, we only really had theories and assumptions as to how things actually occurred; referring to transmissions within the brain via combinations of chemicals and electricity and involving all manner of interrelated processes. Electrical pulses in the brain released neurotransmitters of various types, with the potential to cross the cell membrane into the synaptic gap; the space between two neurons.

Synapses were the connecting points between brain cells; billions of them and therefore trillions of synapses would assist cells to communicate with one another. This affected the voltage of the initially charged neuron, which then created an electrical signal from the receiving neuron. The whole process took less than one five-hundredth of a second to carry out and was in effect how a message was converted within the brain; the thought-trail extrapolated by repetition encompassing more and more neuron to neuron connections; electrical signals transforming into chemical signals and back again and the chain created across the synapses, the basis of all brain activity.

What had been agreed was that the greater the number of signals sent between two neurons, the stronger the invisible bond between them; the result of an additional new experience perhaps or remembering an event or fact and retrieving it from the bank of memories stored. In fact, the brain's memory was akin to a plethora of separate series circuits of Christmas tree lights, where the person's ability to recall a memory would increase the voltage at the source (the initial bond) and enable more lights along that corresponding row to be lit; those additional lights representing other parts of the same memory being brought into the conscience of the person at that exact moment. It was through each of these separate and continuous processes that the brain was constantly evolving; re-wiring its physical structure.

As to why someone was able to recall memories better than others or to remember more, was a different matter all together; Dreamex explaining it through the person's ability to navigate more readily and extensively through each and every one of their sets of Christmas tree lights; a facet like all others that set us apart from each other. The size of the hippocampus provided the limitations or physical parameters to store the lights but there were those who could arrange them more practically and fit more in; therefore not an exact correlation or science. It seemed like a trivial way to explain the workings of the brain's storage and access to memory, Jared thought, but at least it made sense to him.

In addition to neurons, the presentation explained that the brain contained an equal mass of glial cells. Research over the past five years by Dreamex had discovered that the number of these cells was linked to the occurrence and complexity of dreams, not just to the brain's communication and neuroplasticity (the ability of the brain to form and reorganize synaptic connections). They found that there was a much greater concentration of glial cells in those individuals who had a more active brain during unconsciousness; and it was these cells that would continue to stimulate the neurons, causing electrical pulses to dart around the cranial member during sleep. If the electrical pulses passed through the hippocampus; it would then likely re-awaken their short-term and most recently retrieved conscious and subconscious data, which still carried a greater electrical charge; causing the subject to experience the sensation of watching a randomly generated vignette based on the ingredients of their previous interactions; and what we knew as dreams.

Many people past and present have tried to understand why we dream and what, if anything, is the purpose of them. One theory held is that they help us to store important memories and new things we've learned; deleting unimportant or redundant memories, and allowing our conscience to reach a state of equilibrium, given the complicated thoughts and feelings we've amassed and haven't had chance to fully consider in our waking lives.

Research carried out proved that dreams are important to mental and physical health, emotional well-being as well as highlighting sleep disorders that can occur during Rapid Eye Movement or REM sleep, including sleep paralysis and sleep behaviour disorder.

Dreamex described the reoccurrence of dreams where the glial cells had formed a well trodden path through the hippocampus; the electrical pulses finding their way through the same route time after time, given it was one of least resistance. It proved how much that particular series of thoughts had impacted on the subject; its continual presence in their short to mid-term memory; hence more likely to be negative or upsetting, like the death of a loved one or of trauma they faced during their childhood; and commonly known as a nightmare.

Having touched on dreams; they then showed clips from popular films which had centred on the concept; Blade Runner with its 'Replicants' based on Philip K. Dick's 'Do Androids Dream of Electric Sheep?' and Total Recall, which had also created self-doubting characters through the pretext of artificial dreams following implanted memories.

Dreamex were about to raise the stakes though; keen to point out that although many had written about the subject or had created science-fiction on the silver-screen based on it; nobody had actually made much headway on the topic in real terms or been able to replicate the various hypotheses. That was until now...

'Following extensive research and experimentation over the past five years; here at Dreamex, we can now take you even further than Science Fiction itself...Dreamex are proud to present to you 'The Dream Watcher'...

CHAPTER 7

There was a pause in the narration and the holographic images disappeared from above the stage, leaving everyone watching on in a state of intense anticipation at what they were about to discover.

Suddenly, new images appeared; a person asleep and wearing what looked like a hood embossed with numerous thin metallic probes and a machine on the bedside table next to them; a very slim and sleek looking black box with a generic interpretation of the human brain engraved into the top, which was lit up in brilliant neon blue.

'You are witnessing the most technological advance in the history of our time on Earth... and what will soon become the most sought after piece of equipment. This highly sophisticated system is not only able to interpret your hallucinations during sleep but can replicate them on screen for you to watch when you wake... The Dream Watcher...never lose track of your dreams.'

There was a collective gasp and eyes opened wide in response to Dreamex's advertising slogan; the claim they were making was incredible.

At that point the lights came on and Alexander Van Tam stood centre stage alone; a ripple of applause rang out from those watching-on; Jared joining in, wanting to appear as enthusiastic as the others. Once the clapping had subsided following the CEO's raised hand of appreciation, he began to speak to them all.

'I used to have a recurring dream, a good dream; an enjoyable dream...but I was having difficulty describing it to a friend...as you know in dreams, it rarely makes sense in terms of continuity or relativity. People you talk to one second suddenly becoming somebody else the next and yet it all seems very normal and without confusion; also moving from one place to another that were in no way linked or connected. After struggling to explain the dream to a friend whilst enjoying a coffee one lunch-time back in 2027, I said. 'If only you could see it yourself, then you would know what I was talking about.' That statement resonated with me immediately becoming a very real passion of mine and I quickly scribbled down a drawing on the back of a serviette. That was my Eureka moment and I began looking into the science of the brain and how and why dreams actually occurred...

The idea for the Dream Watcher came about after Cinemax patented the technology to superimpose someone into a famous film...you've probably already heard about it. By capturing their facial expressions and body shape on a green-screen, which had become commonplace for CGI in movies, and having them narrate all the corresponding lines from the script; they were then able to cast Joe Public in their own version of their favourite film.

We believed that if you could appear in someone else's creation, then why not your own which was personal to you? Dreams have always been a medium deriving intrigue for a great number of people as well as scientists, so we decided to research the idea with the purpose of capturing them on celluloid...

But we know that dreams cannot be controlled by the dreamer. It's subconscious as well as conscious thoughts interrelating with all manner of things throughout the day which produces them; some of it known but other parts the senses having picked-up but not necessarily dwelt on; like flicking through a picture book and only really noticing a few of the pages. It's normal for some of us to be able to recall and link recent events that appear within our dreams and that realising the fact enables us to move on and let go of them. However, sometimes we cannot always find the link, such as cases where the seeds have been planted subconsciously and therefore we're never able to rationalise the reasons behind them. A person's dreams can tell us more about who they are; no pretences or hiding from the truth as it's their subconscious that is the key to their soul...

It took five years of research to come up with a real breakthrough, which enabled me to build these new headquarters that you're now sitting in. I was confident we could forge a path forward and create something, which had only been a dream itself back then...

A few minutes ago, we all saw a simplified lesson on how our brains work. Well, here at Dreamex, our new invention, The Dream Watcher, interprets patterns of synapses triggered in the brain and is able to correlate different brain synapse trails with that of a differing representation or 'thought object', whatever the person was thinking, whether a physical shape, colour or feeling.'

Van Tam paused. ...

"That's why we need you! All of you have something in common...greater than average brain activity; which is ideal for what we need. Using vivid dreamers like you will enable us to catalogue a complete palette of colours, objects, feelings and much much more. Individual thoughts that the computer software interprets from someone's generic synapse patterns can then be processed as images onto a 2D-screen, thereby enabling them to be recorded. We've called this catalogue of thoughts 'The Dream Vault'...

You will all be paid well as the job advert stated. It's a strange one I know, but here at Dreamex we won't mind at all if we find you asleep on the job...'

A sudden ripple of laughter broke the silence in the auditorium. ...

'And we won't be too bothered about you turning up late for work either...as long as you've saved your dream data onto this; a 'Dream Card'; a memory disk like no other, which can cast its contents remotely onto any device which uses next generation Bluetooth technology,' Van Tam exclaimed whilst holding up an example of the newly-invented hardware.

'Every morning when you arrive, you'll be asked to hand in your 'Dream Card' so we can add its contents to the main Super Computer, which can then be researched by our data-miners. You'll also be given certain tests and tasks to perform...for purely scientific purposes and in order for us to learn more about individuals' brain processes...

But I haven't told you the whole story...you could say I've saved the best till last.'

CHAPTER 8

The 14 Dreamers looked around at each other, finding it hard to believe there could be anything to better what Van Tam had already disclosed, having caused a visceral bewilderment amongst the majority.

Dreamex's CEO then clicked his fingers twice in quick succession; the lights in the main hall and above the audience doubling in brightness. He then walked down the steps from the stage and approached the Dreamers sat on the front row.

'Can you please tell me your names?' he asked, standing in front of a couple, his smile like that of a magician about to carry out a trick and choosing his volunteers.

'David and Chantelle…great…for the benefit of all of the others here, can you please look at me closely and tell everyone what I'm wearing, and if you notice anything strange about me…keep it clean though, as remember; this is a family show.'

After laughing out of embarrassment at having been selected, the pair observed the head of Dreamex Corporation, looking him up and down slowly. They weren't exactly sure what they were looking for and they didn't want to make themselves look stupid in front of their peers.

'Well?' Van Tam announced.

A couple of seconds later, Chantelle broke the silence; 'You're wearing a nice suit.'

The rest of the audience, including David and Van Tam, laughed at her response.

'Well, thank you Chantelle...you're looking very nice in...whatever you're wearing', his reply receiving an even greater volume of laughter.

'Anything else?'

David now weighed in, having spent a little more time considering his own observations. 'You're not wearing a tie.'

'Correct David, but not what I was looking for.'

'You look pretty normal to me,' Chantelle interjected again not having a clue as to what they were supposed to be seeing or not seeing and what was apparently different.

'I'll let you both off, because I wouldn't expect even the most eagle-eyed person to notice,' Van Tam exclaimed and now returned to the stage, a ripple of whispers amongst the audience members as he did so.

A large screen behind him then switched on, and the audience were surprised to note that some of them were now being shown live as they sat there, perplexed as to where the camera filming them was located.

'You are seeing exactly what I am seeing through my eyes right now,' Van Tam announced; the idea seeming so ludicrous that there were more sounds of confusion from the dumbfounded Dreamers looking on.

'Yes, I am wearing the contact lenses of the future...each one with a built-in micro-camera and hence why you are able to view what I can see. The cameras are minute, with a diameter of 2.8mm, no larger or different to that of a nevus or brown spot, which are like naturally occurring freckles found in the whites of the eye, and which do not cause permanent damage or any loss in vision. As you can see; they are almost invisible to the naked eye, and they do not affect the wearer as each camera is positioned over the blind-spot or where the optic nerve attaches to the eye from the brain. The new cameras are using the same technology found in MSCs or micro-scopic-chips; able to carry out millions of calculations and only the size of a pinhead…

These cameras can continuously record information which is sent remotely to the 'Dream Watcher'; the main hard drive that will sit next to your bed and which houses memory ten-times larger than the recently released PS8 from Sony; large enough to store up to 672 hours or four weeks of new FL-IF Diamond-Clear film. The tiny cameras use the same technology as the remote security cameras outside your front door, live streaming data sent via the 7G network and received by our new piece of tech…

I realise you haven't had much time to consider the uses of such technology…but I assure you they are limitless. For the first time ever, a person can now choose to watch their 'real life' day as captured by the cameras too… like a holiday video, able to find the man or woman you saw at the shops that you liked but couldn't remember their face exactly; the document you read at work but had forgotten the contents and anything else that you may not have given your fullest attentions to during your day…a security camera or dash-cam for the eyes but without anyone else knowing or able to notice them…

You will understand why we ensured not to tell you anything about our new invention before you signed NDAs and your contracts. This is top secret information; especially as the technology could be used in so many different ways; such as in the military, medical surgery, the police or sports entertainment. Imagine being able to see the view from the footballers' own perspective on the pitch or leading up to a goal, the armchair fan being able to select the live feed from his favourite player and even during the highlights...and that's just football. Its uses are endless...and I haven't mentioned the most practical uses; those on holiday capturing memories together, a couple seeing how the other sees them at exactly the same moment, and other special events like weddings...without needing a camera or a phone...just being able to enjoy yourselves and look back through the video later; able to edit it with ease using the Dream Watcher's 'Eye-Spy' software...

The same technical department that created the contact lens cameras on the third-floor here at Dreamex are currently working on a compatible microphone, which we hope will be completed in the next couple of months. This auxiliary information will then create the ultimate experience for everyone who chooses to use the Dream Watcher...but I haven't told you why we have invented these contact lenses...

Those more astute amongst you may have asked yourself what these contact lens cameras have to do with a machine which was in effect, first and foremost, created to interpret and record people's dreams...and I'd be saying 'that's a great question'. Well I'll tell you...

The video captured by the contact lens cameras doesn't just work in tandem with the Dream Watcher whilst the person is awake but it provides their real time memory when they are asleep and connected via the 'Dream Cap'. As the system reads a person's individual brain synapse activity during sleep, it is not only able to determine what the person is thinking from the 'Dream Vault' but it is able to pinpoint an exact object/person/thought given the best match within their real time daily recordings over the previous month;

some of which they may not have realised at the time but that their subconscious and the contact lens cameras picked-up...

The system software is so advanced it can substitute real video objects, caught through Eye-Spy lenses, for that conjured up through the synapse pattern correlation within the Dream Vault...and splice it together so effectively that it produces a seamless video; with no distortion and giving an almost identical replica of the person's dream or something we're confident that will closely resemble it...

The need for the Eye-Spy lenses is to ensure that the individual's own Dream Watcher shows the correct version of the thought object relative to the dreamer as, for example, one person's vision of an elephant within their memory bank may be completely different to that of another person's.

In order to further increase the accuracy of results, each new system can be calibrated by the new owner at initial start-up. This is achieved by asking the customer, slash wearer, to think of particular objects when connected up via the Dream Cap...such as an elephant, Marilyn Monroe or the colour blue...there are literally hundreds of these examples which are carried out so as for the Dream Watcher to discern and therefore tailor its results to the individuals' own synapse patterns in addition to the Dream Vault portmanteau of objects already in place; and which you will help increase via our continued R&D...the calibration will not only increase the accuracy of the system on a person by person basis but will also be able to detect their personal tastes and idiosyncrasies... Further still; the developed software has built-in 'clever technology' that can adapt to the individual over time, given that we all change our opinions and prioritise things differently as we get older...

We're hoping to have the final prototype ready for sale by Christmas 2042; which although I appreciate seems a while off; it will only be with your help that we can achieve this goal...oh and one thing I must stress...there will be severe punishments handed out in the event that any of this information is leaked, and is the reason why you were all told not to bring anything that could be used to record or transmit any information that you've witnessed here today...and just in case you were wondering how we would know...you were all scanned on entering the lifts...

However, we are confident that you will be as excited as us to be helping with this project and to be a part of this world first concept...Oh and if you were wondering; we are in the midst of completing the very detailed submission to the Patent Office...once the Dream Watcher technology is rubber-stamped, then the lid can come off the box and we will start our global marketing strategy; although I have purposely dropped some crumbs of interest amongst some of the technology conference goers and hinted at big future revelations to reporters working for tech journals...

Until the patent has been made official; all equipment will remain on these premises and all testing carried out here, as we don't want anyone getting their hands on it before then. However, once this has been received, you will each be kitted out with a first-gen Dream Watcher to take home with you, which will make capturing the data more practical.'

Chapter 9

After Van Tam had finished his long and detailed monologue; he asked if anybody had any questions. Given what they had just learnt about Dreamex and the Dream Watcher, there was a lot for them to take in and far too early for any of them to consider asking anything further at that stage.

Now that all the lights had come on, Jared could focus his attentions on the girl sat on the row in front of him. He'd noticed her earlier in the lift and was very pleased to see that she'd also made it through as a Dreamer.

As Van Tam brought things to a close, confirming that everyone would start the following Monday at 9am, he left the stage from the back. The audience now had the opportunity to discuss what they'd just witnessed.

Jared made a beeline for the girl who had caught his eye as she started making her way up the steps towards the exit.

'What did you make of that, then?' he asked enthusiastically having caught up with her.

Stopping and turning to face him; the two now looked briefly at each other. Jared was woeful at remaining calm in such circumstances, piling pressure on himself to make a good first impression, and yet at the same time readying himself for disappointment; usually finding out that the woman was already in a relationship.

His luck had indeed been quite poor when it came to finding a partner; his last episode having gone the same route as most; when having noticed a girl who worked for a firm next door to him at the Bank. The pair would find themselves waiting for the bus to the Park and Ride most evenings and Jared was left thinking she was interested as she would always choose to smile at him; although there was never any actual conversation.

As Jared wrestled with confidence issues, based on his previous experience; he decided to push himself into making an effort. One evening after work he decided to write a note on a slip of paper, which read 'I really like you. My name is Jared. If you fancy going for a drink sometime then give me a call' and leaving his number at the bottom. So far so good he thought, but he still had to make sure she got the note.

Walking to the bus stop after work as usual; there she was. She was even more beautiful than he'd remembered and his insides were going crazy with anxiety, all hot and flustered and questioning his rather forward plan. He convinced himself to continue; besides; what was the worst thing that could happen?

Unfortunately, there were quite a few more people queuing that night, which made handing her the note a much greater dilemma. Then, as the bus turned up and parked adjacent to them; Jared moved to the front of the queue and to the girl, who was just about to step onto it. 'Excuse me…I think you just dropped this,' he exclaimed passing her his note. He'd done it. He was pleased with himself for having carried it out, but the feeling was short-lived; immediately superseded by that of dread as she now knew he liked her, and there was no hiding from it any more.

Jared didn't receive any phone call or message that evening; convinced that his idea had been futile and there was no way someone so good-looking would be interested in him after all.

The next day after work; Jared was fully aware that he now had to run the embarrassing gauntlet of catching the bus again, and there was a good chance there would be someone else waiting there also. He sheepishly made his way to the stop and as he rounded the bend in the road; there she was; waiting in her usual position. Jared walked with an air of forced confidence. However, just as he was approaching and readying himself for an awkward acknowledgement; a car pulled up next to her and she got in, not looking at Jared as she did so. It appeared evident that she was not interested in him whatsoever, kissing her boyfriend who was the driver, a man that looked bigger than Bluto from Popeye and left Jared feeling like a complete fool.

***

'Hi' she replied, somewhat surprised at Jared's question. 'All very futuristic isn't it?' she continued now carrying on climbing the steps and with Jared doing likewise behind, ensuring not to clip her heels.

'My name's Jared by the way…I guess we'll be seeing a lot more of each other from now on…so thought I'd introduce myself.'

'Right…nice to meet you Jared…I'm Lorna.'

As the pair reached the corridor outside the conference auditorium; another girl butted in and started speaking with Lorna, the two chatting as though they'd known each other for some time. Jared was left hanging; thinking she wasn't interested at all or certainly not wishing to spend any more time conversing with him. Jared licked his wounds yet again and returned home. However, it was the concept of the

Dream Watcher that occupied his mind more so than Lorna and he couldn't wait to begin work at Dreamex.

Chapter 10

Jared loved his new job and getting to know everyone at the company, including the other Dreamers, especially Lorna. Although their relationship had remained strictly platonic, Jared could not change the fact that he was still very attracted to her and his days were very much improved with her in them; disappointed when they were not on the same shift together.

It wasn't just Lorna that affected his work-life as Jared became well liked by everyone, his positive and somewhat original sense of humour resonating well with them all. Being well-liked came with benefits too, as it was the result of who he was and not any planned act on his part. Because he was reliable above everything else; he gained the trust of the lead scientists and even Van Tam himself, who promoted Jared to head of Dreamers within six months. He was now spending more time in the boardroom, at extra-curricular functions and meetings; an ideal candidate for representing the company, with his politeness and obvious integrity.

Having spent his first two years supplying dream data as one of the 32 Dreamers and representing his colleagues; Van Tam had been impressed with Jared's ideas and his understanding of the concept, despite lacking previous scientific experience. He had a mathematical mind, a vivid imagination and a way with words, making him a very valuable commodity and one that Van Tam was keenly aware of.

Jared was therefore further promoted to assist the Business Development Manager at Dreamex shortly after, leaving the Dreamers and Lorna to their daily tasks and now located on the first floor in the executive offices; only a short walk from the CEO's luxury pad. Jared's relationship with Van Tam had developed enormously; so much so that he'd ask Jared to carry out the occasional task for him; akin to a personal assistant role. Jared was a little nonplussed at times with handling, what were in effect, Van Tam's personal dealings, but realised the significance of him being called upon to help.

Having seen a somewhat meteoric rise up the hierarchy, Jared believed it might cause Lorna to have second thoughts about him; especially as he was now effectively rubbing shoulders with the big guns at the company and got to hear of new developments and other interesting issues before others. However, despite not letting his new role affect the way in which he treated everyone; Lorna did not seem as impressed with him as he'd hoped. Knowing his continued pursuit of her could jeopardise his position, Jared came to the conclusion that he'd have to give up on her and leave well alone.

Following the issue of the patent regarding the Dream Watcher and its related science, Jared had received a first prototype to take home with him as was mentioned initially by Van Tam after passing his audition. He'd been thrilled to be one of only a handful to now have the tech in his possession and was quick to set it up. Dreamex had been keen to facilitate this; knowing they would greatly increase data through their Dreamers' natural sleeping patterns; their Dream Cards providing much more information which could be stored in the main Super Computer.

Fitting the Eye-Spy lenses was no problem for Jared either; having worn contacts from the age of seventeen to aid him with playing sport, before corrective lasers had become so ultra efficient and reliable that having his vision corrected had no longer been a cause for concern. Jared had also noticed an indirect benefit of wearing lenses in his youth, as it increased his confidence greatly, which in turn made him a more attractive proposition to the opposite sex.

Van Tam had made it very clear from the outset that no one entrusted with the equipment outside would be allowed to wear the lenses on Dreamex premises. He did not want any video to be passed onto or viewed by others and enable them to see how the company operated. There were hundreds of scanners in the building which could detect the presence of the Eye-Spy technology in case someone tried to defy the rules or had simply forgotten that they were wearing them; the lenses able to remain in the eye overnight due to the breathable material they were made from.

Jared set up the Dream Watcher hard drive next to his bed; the Dream Card already inserted as shown by the red light on the readout display. With the Dream Cap stowed under his pillow and having already configured the unit whilst first having used it at work; he was ready to go. He could now record his dreams from the comfort of his own bedroom and it felt like a massive leap forwards; akin to being allowed to take the class pet home for the holidays.

He'd been thinking about playing back his dreams at home for some time. He was not content with just casting it to his tablet but wanted to see what it looked like through his 3D/HD projector in his cinema room on the second floor of his house. The image beamed onto a white wall and providing a 120-inch viewable area, the measurement representing the diagonal and so around 72 inches high and 96 wide. It was then easy for Jared to feel immersed in the action, lying back on his sofa; some three metres from the 'screen'.

Dreamex were still working on an app to aid connectivity to more home-entertainment peripherals and the next generation mobile-phone technology; also enabling streaming via social media; but for now it was the plug-and-play of old. Jared knew his projector was a little dated compared to the holographic sets you could now purchase, but they were a little outside his budget and he preferred the feel of his more traditional set-up.

Everything was turning out better than Dreamex could ever have imagined; ahead of schedule with the development of the Dream Vault thanks to the Dreamers and all the separate parts of the system were coming together nicely. Nothing it seemed could thwart their momentum; the general consensus reflected by the strong share price from aggressive purchasing; speculators aware of the potential long-term gains to be made. However, as was almost always customary with new ventures; they wouldn't have it all their own way; and one day they were faced with a dilemma that jeopardised the entire future of the Dream Watcher.

CHAPTER 11

It was just a normal day at Dreamex; Jared having arrived half an hour early to take advantage of the breakfast menu in the staff restaurant. After finishing his scrambled egg stuffed crumpets and making his way along the corridor to his office he was alarmed to see some of the executive staff and lead scientists running towards him, almost knocking him over and all wearing serious expressions.

'What's going on?' Jared called out loudly so as to be heard over the commotion.

'We've got a problem with one of the Dreamers,' his colleague replied, continuing to make haste for the lifts.

Jared dropped his bag and jacket just inside his office, before running after them; filled with trepidation at what he might discover when he got there.

Catching up with the others on the fourth floor, it was obvious where the incident had taken place; a large number of people congregated outside testing-lab five. A Dreamer Jared recognised was being comforted by some of the others. Managing to cut through the mêlée, he made his way into the monitoring room which annexed it; two scientists were sitting despondently showing very little emotion; one having leant forward, propping himself up with his elbows on the desk in front of him; both hands placed on top of his head as he looked down. The other stared blankly through the two-way mirror and Jared now turned to do likewise.

There were a number of Dreamex medics around one of the dentist chairs; each of them looking dejected and the room was littered with all kinds of medical cardio-equipment. The body of one of the Dreamers lay prone, shrouded in a blanket. A group of executives including Van Tam were standing several feet away from the morbid scene and looking deeply concerned; the CEO acknowledging to the medics that they had each done their best.

Jared suddenly felt cold; physically sick to the stomach; not knowing who lay beneath the blanket had sent a rush of negative adrenaline coursing through him; his anxiety levels off the chart; the shock could not have been greater. Although having shifted into Business Development, he'd got to know all of the Dreamers well over the last five years, especially having started out as one himself. For someone to lose their life was the most serious of outcomes and he thought of those whom he'd got on best with. Although it seemed selfish, he hoped it was none of them. He was keenly aware that the affect on him would depend entirely on whomever it was that had died.

Jared realised the monitors in front of him had the names of the Dreamers attached to them for research purposes. But he was reluctant to bring himself to look. After a short pause he began opening his eyes slowly and peered down at the monitor...it was Lorna.

Jared was inconsolable. He'd always felt an affinity towards Lorna since noticing her at the auditions and through their interactions ever since; although obvious she didn't feel the same way about him. Their friendship had developed greatly nonetheless and he'd still have given anything to be with her. It seemed incredible that out of all of the Dreamers it had to be Lorna that had gone. There was suddenly an enormous void in his life; the extent to which Lorna would not have known, given Jared had never expressed his true feelings to her. His life would feel very different from now on.

    Arriving home, still numb from what had happened, Jared found himself automatically making his way to his bedroom, placing his bag on his single bed before sitting at his piano next to it. He had always found solace in music; a way for him to express his emotions, which he would otherwise keep very much to himself. Placing his fingers on the keys, he paused briefly; remembering Lorna; and after a minute or so began to play Traumerei by Schumann, one of thirteen pieces making up Scenes from Childhood, and coincidentally based on dreams.

    Jared could not help but dwell on the emotive tone his playing evoked; his thoughts picking out memories of Lorna that affected him most; like a perfectly choreographed montage of sadness depicted in a movie or poignant photographs of the deceased displayed during a funeral service and leaving no one with a dry eye in the congregation.

    It had always been one of his favourite pieces to play; relatively short and one of the simplest he knew, but in its simplicity came with it one of the most beautiful melodies, conjuring up a raw sense of loss like no other and demanding self-reflection for the time it would last. Jared continued, the tears forming in his eyes began hazing his sight and causing him to blink, as he remembered Lorna. His feelings playing out through the most heartfelt version he'd ever produced. When the final note dissipated to silence, Jared sat very still as his tears continued to flow.

CHAPTER 12

Although it seemed wrong, Dreamex covered up Lorna's death to ensure it never made it into the news or onto social media. The finished prototype of the Dream Watcher was not far from completion and they realised how much of a negative impact it would have; not just on the continuation of the project but its knock-on effect on future sales.

They had to cover up Lorna's death as it was the technology behind the Dream Watcher that had been responsible, not natural causes. Jared had learnt of this from Van Tam himself, having barged into his room the next day; passionate to find out what had happened and wanting to get to the bottom of it.

Van Tam had a great deal of respect for Jared and decided to confide in him, explaining the weird phenomenon that had led to Lorna's death.

'Okay Jared...just calm down; I know what happened to Lorna was terrible; everyone is shocked and upset. It's a major setback to the project that we've all put so much effort into and we need to learn lessons from it.'

'Setback? Someone lost their life yesterday...I'd say it was a little more important than that,' Jared replied angrily as he sat on a chair glaring at Van Tam.

'I appreciate that Jared...but in the whole scheme of things, such occurrences have thankfully not been too frequent.'

'Not been too frequent? You mean to tell me this has happened before?' Jared exclaimed with alarm.

Van Tam took a few seconds to mull over what he was going to say...and then began explaining what he meant.

'Okay Jared; I'll level with you...when the software was in its infancy and we began initial testing; there were some teething problems...we lost two employees within the space of a fortnight...we didn't know it could happen...otherwise we would have done something about it...but like in many other projects; whether in transportation, construction or even science, there are statistically always going to be some fatalities...

It's terrible I realise that...and nobody wants it to happen...but we knew we couldn't just give up on the project as a result...it's much bigger than the deaths of two...now three people...call it unfortunate collateral damage but it's a fact of life...it's sadly how we learn in a lot of cases; to improve the processes and make them safer in the future...to prevent it from happening ever again. We thought we'd managed to do that; but yesterday proved there's still a risk.'

'What teething problems...prevent what from happening again? What happened?'

Van Tam looked a little uncomfortable and seemed to be at pains to admit anything else; but eventually he responded.

'Well we assumed the first death had been due to natural causes; an epileptic fit or the like and they'd swallowed their tongue...however, with the second death happening in a similar fashion so soon after, we realised there must have been a connection with the system we'd created...we therefore spent hundreds of man hours investigating...it was touch and go at one stage whether we scrapped the whole concept and started again. Our scientists finally got to the bottom of it after researching the data and patterns of brain activity in both incidents leading up to their deaths, and were able to successfully pinpoint the cause.

Jared listened intently to Van Tam, eyes fixed on him, desperate to learn of the reason for Lorna's death.

CHAPTER 13

'You see, Jared, there's an inbuilt function in our brains that produces a condition known as atonia; a mechanism which places the body's muscles in a temporary state of paralysis during REM sleep, the deepest part of sleep and when we're most likely to experience dreaming. Despite believing our dreams are real at that specific moment and continuing to initiate physiological commands in reaction to them; the paralysis prevents us from physically acting anything out. There are those for whom atonia levels aren't as efficient as others though... and it's these people who are prone to sleepwalking or behavioural disorders; such as kicking out during sleep, with some even having been known to attack their partners in bed next to them without even realising it.'

'So, are you saying that Lorna and these other two didn't have sufficient atonia and therefore somehow just went berserk?' Jared asked with a puzzled expression on his face.

'It's true that there appears to be a link between the deficiency of someone's atonia that exacerbates their deaths in this way...on closer inspection of the corresponding video and data, however, we learnt of a new phenomena called a 'dream-vortex', something that none of us could ever have foreseen....

As the Dream Watcher records people's dreams, we didn't envisage that people would spend so much time watching their own dreams that they would then potentially begin to dream about the process of watching their own dreams. This was the state in which the two previous Dreamers and now Lorna had entered...and as we've seen has proved to be fatal.'

'So what happened to them then...in this vortex?'

'We don't understand exactly what happens to trigger the vortex in a physiological sense...but it appears that once the mind enters this state it creates an infinite loop, and there is no way for someone to exit from it. It causes their whole body to spasm which is in direct contrast to their atonia that tries to prevent it; like literally switching every single one of their functions on and off at the same time over and over again...and the host is no longer able to take back control of their own brain...

As it powers the body's autonomic nervous system, responsible for all processes that usually take place without our conscious effort; such as regulating blood pressure, heart rate, body temperature and of breathing itself; then all these suddenly become erratic. Within seconds of these processes breaking down, they lose their ability to function normally and makes it impossible for the person to survive...CPR has proven futile, even if successful, as they are in effect brain dead.'

Jared looked shocked. The idea that Lorna had been through what Van Tam had just explained was truly horrifying and there was little he could think about other than that. He was speechless. The Dreamex CEO, noticing his demeanour, continued to explain what had happened previously.

'Following the first two fatalities; our scientists made some important additions to the technology; inventing a built-in wake-up switch which would be triggered if the machine detected that the Dreamer was beginning to recall the act of viewing previous dreams or the process of having their dreams being recorded in the test-lab…basically the machine would intervene to halt a repeat of the dream-vortex before it had a chance to begin. We thought we'd fixed the problem for good…but Lorna's death, yesterday, confirmed it was still possible.'

'Well, there's no way you can sell the Dream Watcher to millions of people if it can potentially kill them…no matter how infrequent or unlikely it is of happening.'…

'Like I said, Jared…as terrible as Lorna's death is; I'm not going to pull the plug on the whole project because of it…we need to carry out a further investigation…of course I'm not going to give the green light for releasing it until I'm 100% sure it's safe to do so…I hope you can understand why we need to keep what just happened away from the media; any mention of this outside these walls and it has the potential to completely ruin everything. Nothing has changed in my eyes…the Dream Watcher will still become the most famous invention of all time and propel this company to the very top…there's no question about it.'

Jared was unhappy at what he'd heard; angered that he and 31 other Dreamers had been put in mortal danger without even realising it. There was a lot for him to consider and not least Lorna and how her death would be reported. He knew things were very raw right now and that he would have to toe the company line if he wanted to remain there; a job he'd loved for the last five years and the security it provided him. He was distraught about Lorna but did not want to walk away from Dreamex. He'd invested too much time and effort in the company and still wanted to play a big part in it; and besides, he realised how tough it would be to find another job.

CHAPTER 14

It was a difficult few days at Dreamex following Lorna's death; the other Dreamers given a couple of weeks off on full pay but were never told what really happened to her. Jared found it extremely difficult to deal with; thinking about her a lot; especially at work, where he'd been so used to seeing her, mostly because he'd gone out of his way to ensure that he did.

It was no surprise that Jared was not only thinking about Lorna during his waking hours but during his dreams too. This gave him the opportunity to see her again; starring in his own creations, in life-size on his large projection screen, but it made his sense of loss seem even more acute. He'd captured her beauty and smile time after time and night after night in whatever scenario his subconscious memory imagined.

Then, one Saturday morning, after spending a little more time in bed after a late night; he woke, removing his Dream Cap and recalling the vivid dream he'd had. It felt like he'd literally just experienced it. Keener than ever to watch it again, he ejected the Dream Card from the Dream Watcher and quickly made his way upstairs.

Entering the cinema room, he inserted the card into his media tower, before blocking out the daylight piercing through the skylights by drawing the blinds; sitting back on the sofa and waiting for the data files to populate on screen. There were three separate dream episodes that had been picked up by the Dream Watcher during the night; two only 3-4 minutes long but it was the longer one at nearly 17-

minutes that he scrolled to and clicked on; knowing it was the likeliest one, and the one he hoped he'd remembered most vividly. After pressing play, there was a momentary pause as the Dreamex logo pulsed at the centre of the screen before the images from his unconscious thoughts appeared.

He was in the entrance at the Dreamex Corporation; although it seemed much bigger than in reality, his obvious take on how large he'd initially thought of the space having been exaggerated as was common in dreams. He seemed lost; unsure about where things were, despite knowing his way around every part of the building in reality. Jared assumed it was he who was lost; the feelings that he'd felt during the actual event not able to be fully portrayed, despite the view from his own perspective and what he could see through his own eyes.

Jared looked around more desperately now but the entrance was no longer there; the whole facade bricked over and he felt them with his hand, checking if they were real. Then, he noticed her; Lorna, across the other side of the entrance hall at the bottom of the sweeping staircase and she was wearing the finest red dress he'd ever seen, reaching all the way to the floor, covering all of her body, except for her shoulders and magnificent cleavage.

She was staring right at Jared, her eyes increasing in size as she seemed besotted with him; never having looked at him in that way before. She smiled; her lips coated brilliant crimson and after raising her arm out in front of her, beckoned Jared towards her with her fingers in a rhythmical and sensual movement.

Jared watched from his sofa, captivated by Lorna on the screen in front of him; infatuated by her, but also having to fight with his own conscience; a conscience which was reminding him that it was perhaps wrong to be deriving such animalistic pleasure given what had happened to her only eight days before.

As Jared remembered more of the dream as he saw it come to life in front of his eyes; the temptation to continue watching Lorna was too difficult to ignore as she started walking up the steps slowly, looking over her shoulder at him; Jared now stood at the foot of the stairs looking up at her. Suddenly, in his dream, the view shifted to the monitor that was recording Lorna's dreams in test-lab five, showing her brain activity starting to flicker unnaturally from the norm like a seismograph picking up on some sudden earth tremors.

The picture then returned to Lorna ascending the staircase, having traversed a few more steps by now, the red dress having disappeared; Lorna wearing nothing more than her underwear and suspenders. Again, the picture changed back to the test-lab as her body went into spasms in the dentist chair; alarms going off, although the alarms didn't sound like anything he'd heard at Dreamex.

Returning to the stairs once again, Lorna was naked, her body from behind was perfect, just as it was in Jared's imagination, having never actually seen her like that before. She was now gesticulating to him and Jared was following her even more closely. As she reached the top of the stairs, she began turning slowly to face him...and now he could see all of her...

The image suddenly disappeared leaving a white screen illuminated on the wall in front of him. Jared had pressed the stand-by button on the remote and threw it onto the sofa seat on the other side of the room. He'd been hovering his finger above it since he'd first seen Lorna on-screen; his conscience having got the better of him and knowing it was wrong to keep watching, especially as he was keenly aware of what was about to happen.

Getting to his feet; Jared turned everything off, and after releasing the blinds made his way down the two flights of stairs to the kitchen to make a coffee. He felt a strange sense of shame on the one hand but still longing to have made love to her on the other. He needed a fix of reality quickly to bring him out of his current state of mind. He hollered to Cindy to turn on the news and then sat there at the breakfast bar with his hot drink trying to regain his composure.

Jared wiped the dream of Lorna from the Dream Card before taking it into work on Monday, aware, on many levels, that it was not something that he wanted the data miners to discover; not least because it seemed wholly inappropriate given what had happened. He realised that his dream data wasn't as rich and plentiful since Lorna's death, but was hoping to return to some semblance of normality; to benefit from a greater variety of dreams that would help him get over his loss.

It was a few days later, after having created a wider selection of less personal dreams to enjoy, that Jared discovered something that could only best be described as unimaginable; something so far removed from reality that it would serve to have a profound effect on him thereafter, and something that meant his life would never be the same again.

CHAPTER 15

Having set up his previous night's dreams to play via his projector; Jared lay back as he had done on many occasions and began watching. This time he hadn't remembered any of them; having tried to cling to a snippet he could recall but having proved unsuccessful in retaining the thread. At least he knew he could be reminded of it; the joys of the Dream Watcher.

Within a few seconds, the screen was populated with a magnificent desertscape; large dunes in the background and a searing bright haze portraying a hot environment. But there was also a stereotypical incarnation of an oasis in the foreground; a cool refreshing spring of water rising from a plunge pool and a variety of colourful flowers and tropical vegetation lining it, now being sprayed by a cool moist mist. It was like something described within the pages of a self-meditation handbook and Jared found it instantly relaxing.

The colours were so vivid and the scene so appetising that Jared suddenly felt a burning desire to get closer and to imagine himself there.

Although realising it was a little bizarre, he got up from the sofa and walked up to the projected image; standing centimetres from it; his frame now completely silhouetted within the parameters of the screen, except that was for his feet and the bottom part of his legs. He had done this after first purchasing the projector when wanting to get a better idea as to the standard of pixel definition and picture quality. He was amazed at how lifelike his dream now appeared in front of him.

Still finding himself lured by his own tranquil creation, he reached out his hand towards it; his brain having already prepared him for the disappointing reality; the certainty that his senses would soon experience despite wishing otherwise...but those feelings never materialised. Jared recoiled his hand immediately as though having touched a naked flame. He was now filled with fear...for his hand had not come into contact with the wall; he'd witnessed his hand appearing inside the image on screen and it was now covered by a moist film. He stared at it; noticing the fresh water droplets. His eyes opened wide with shock. The situation sent unwanted shivers surging through his body like large electric currents; feeling them terminating with real force via every single one of his nerve endings. Jared had entered his own dream.

Convincing himself there was a perfectly good explanation for what had happened; Jared tried to calm himself and come up with reasons to clarify the situation. Perhaps his hand had already been wet or he was still dreaming. But no matter what he came up with, he knew he was awake, impossible as it was to believe.

Realising he would need to repeat what he'd done to prove it was real; Jared tentatively extended his arm towards the screen again, physically shaking. He was scared of having to admit that the logical parameters he'd taken for granted up to that point had been removed, and that was a very disconcerting thought.

Having replayed the dream from the beginning, he decided to reach into the image from the other side of the large projection screen this time and to the flora that lined the oasis, wondering whether he would be able to feel the texture of the leaves or flowering buds. He watched his hand and the lower part of his arm re-enter the dream and appear inside the image near to the vegetation to his utter amazement. Despite feeling anxious, he felt compelled to continue to probe further into the vista, aware that his arm had now disappeared from the room up to his shoulder. It was far more evidence than he needed to prove the phenomenon. There was no doubt whatsoever now.

Jared pulled his arm slowly out from the desert scene and back into the room, checking there was nothing wrong with it. He switched everything off; his mind saturated with feelings and questions that he needed to think about. Was this a side-effect of the Dream Watcher that Dreamex hadn't foreseen or was this something completely personal to him? Could he physically walk into the screen and walk around in his dream world? How would he get back? Would he be able to suffer harm or physical injury and could he enter other dreams, not just this one?

Jared said nothing about his experience to anyone; not even his close friends, and he was certainly not going to mention anything to Van Tam until he'd had chance to answer the multitude of questions his overactive and inquisitive conscience had produced.

In order to try to answer them, Jared experimented over the next few days. He discovered he <u>could</u> enter other dreams but he was not confident enough to fully submerse himself yet, as he didn't know whether he could return to reality safely. In order to take that huge step, Jared knew he would have to confide in someone else.

Troy Skeetman was Jared's best mate; he knew he could trust him with his life; and that seemed like a necessary requirement right now. That was if Troy's presence did not affect his ability to enter his own dream or if Troy could potentially enter it too. So many questions and so much he wanted to test out.

His initial fear and trepidation had slowly been substituted for enthusiasm and a sense of hopeful anticipation; he now wanted to see how far the boundaries of his dream world and his own interaction with them would take him.

CHAPTER 16

72 trillion miles or 12 light-years away from Earth in the Higher Sentient Galaxy, an emergency meeting had been called. His Excellency, Santor Villamott CXXIV, together with the five leaders of the Galactic Colonisation Research Programme had gathered in light of new developments that centred on Jared's discovery.

'Well, it was always going to happen…we knew someone would come along whose imagination would be great enough for them to believe that it was possible…that they could enter their dream world and interact with anyone or anything and by doing so make others believe and bring the two dimensions together.'

'It shouldn't be a surprise…this man's subconscious brain activity at his audition was off the charts; we'd never seen that much glial cell activity or synapse neuroplasticity in any subject tested before…'

'The consequences of his actions are a set-back. We all knew it was imperative that the humans never learnt of this possibility. We will need to shelve it for now and try to integrate the Dream Watcher again at a later stage…but first we need to eradicate the current problem…imagine what effect this would have if left unchecked and how difficult it would be for us to keep track of the project.'

'Well, he might change the course of history within the experiment if we let him continue. It will cause way too much instability.'

'Yes, we need to pull the Dream Watcher for now...it's as simple as that. It's one thing for them to be able to see into one another's minds but it will open up Armageddon if this race has the tools to travel into parallel universes.'

'I disagree,' his Excellency exclaimed, interrupting proceedings. 'Let us observe the hysteria that you suggest will unfold on Earth...it'll be of scientific interest if nothing else and enable us to learn for future projects in other galaxies. This human race has shown how primitive it is; they're incapable of working together, which is what we need to successfully colonise planets and make them work for us. If it gets out of hand then we will intervene...until then, let us see how it plays out.'

'Well, what about the human's impending arrival on Mars? It's difficult enough to watch them making a mess of one planet; let alone allowing them to ruin another.'

'Yes; they haven't come anywhere near solving their own problems. We need to send a team down to sabotage their equipment on Mars; that should set them back at least twenty years.'

'Perhaps making everyone the same colour would have been the easier option from the start and prevented them from needlessly fighting and killing one another.'

'Well, look at Planet Belpergiss in the Hades quadrant...the Bontons haven't all turned on each other due to their obvious differences. I rather think it's to do with personality traits...we need to cut back on giving the humans as much scope next time to develop their emotions. We might lose a little variety but as long as they're intelligent enough to colonise planets for our benefit, without unnecessary infighting, it should be successful.'

'Considering they're all the same race; it's difficult to understand why there are those who treat others with no respect or dignity; even shunning those that are fleeing for their lives. They appear to think that life is a game and they're winning...

We've got a two tier system in operation now; those at the top and bottom, the ones at the top showing no feelings for their fellow race. We haven't seen such an unequal distribution of wealth in any of our previous experiments...

If this is allowed to continue it will only wreak more pain and misery. We've learnt enough about them to know they can never be a positive addition to the universe and in a few decades they won't be able to breathe because of the toxins they've brought upon themselves. They aren't the most intelligent race; that's true; but the pursuit of power and greed by a minority will leave their descendants struggling to survive; we have never seen such a blatant disregard in any of our previous projects; and that includes races with less sentience than these humans.'

'Although we provided them with enough resources to all live comfortably, it seems some just want it all for themselves. Millions of people are not receiving basic nourishment or clean water according to the data and yet there are those who are devising trips to other planets? It's preposterous whichever way you look at it.'

His Excellency interrupted proceedings once again...

'The experiment has shown us that this race has no chance of creating a productive and peaceful colony. We're going to have to release another virus soon if this continues and hope that they finally wake up to the facts that they're all in it together. If things don't start improving in the next ten Earth years, I see no other option than to press the reset button and cancel the project altogether; we can always start over again with a different genus in another galaxy...agreed?'

His Excellency received the backing of all five members of the Counsel and the motion was carried following the unanimous decision.

CHAPTER 17

Having invited Troy over to his house later that evening via the holographic-display phone, known as the holophone, Jared resisted mentioning anything about his discovery, until he had shown him how the Dreamex technology worked. Jared knew if he told Troy that he could enter his own dreams from the start, then it was likely he would freak out.

'Did anyone at Dreamex mention the pitfalls of being able to watch your dreams or to watch other people's dreams?' Troy asked after Jared had shown him the Eye-Spy contact lenses, the Dream Watcher main console at the side of his bed, and the Dream Cap stowed under his pillow.

'I think they deliberately blinkered themselves with their reasoning for developing the Dream Watcher...concentrating on the positives, which I guess is normal for those bringing out new inventions...knowing how much money they could potentially make. It did cross my mind that there were, and are, a lot of moral issues. You're right. I spoke with Van Tam, the CEO, after he promoted me into Business Development; we'd regularly have deep and meaningful conversations about its uses but he always came down on the side of the pros rather than any of the cons.'

'Well the big one that jumps out at me is integrity within a relationship...if a husband or wife watch their partner's dream and see them cheating with someone they work with, the divorce rate would be astronomical. Then there's domestic violence and other related crimes that could result. If these contact lens cameras can record someone's entire waking hours then their partner could be scrutinising that too, which would also lead to increases in voyeurism, up-skirting and stalking.'

'Van Tam mentioned they were going to include a feature that disabled the Dream Watcher from recording anything of a sexual or inappropriate nature...but it's still in the pipeline. You're right; it would get banned within a week if they didn't.'

'They would need to do that, as otherwise it'll be an end to people's free will; having to censor their own behaviour.'

'Yeah; it would turn into an addiction for some wanting to re-watch their days and constantly upload clips on social media. People would be spending their day watching what others were doing, under surveillance from their partners. The drawback to the contact lens cameras are that the person who chooses to watch what they've already seen during their day is in effect duplicating their life, watching themselves on a plus-one channel. They could become so self-centred that the true joy of life would be lost, the wearer doing things through peer pressure and a desire to impress others, rather than leading a normal life and enjoying the highlights along the way.'

'And just imagine how profitable the data would be if Dreamex sold it to the huge multinationals. If these corporations had access to the contact lens camera footage, they could see everything that a person did, ate, spent their time doing, etcetera, and use intelligent marketing campaigns to push tailored products directly at them.'

'I know what you mean. I read about that recently...Intelligent Advertising; it's why there are so many marketing companies springing up everywhere...it's already happening now via people's mobile phones, email and social media accounts. People have no other option than to agree to their terms if they want to use it...advertisers can automatically target them with products based on their interests, location, age, sex and also take into account their likely budget; even down to showing them products in their favourite colour to tempt them. The level of detail is unrivalled; no longer a generic advert but fine-tuned to encourage everyone to buy their product; it all comes down to sharing personal information. Dreamex's potential profits could propel them into one of the largest tech-companies in the world overnight.'

'just imagine how beneficial the data would be to the government too...able to use it to police the country and keep tabs on those claiming benefits...like black boxes fitted to cars to monitor speed and driving behaviour. Life Insurance companies only guaranteeing full premium payouts for those policy holders who wear Eye-Spy cameras and therefore prove their lifestyle and cause of death.'

'Well, I guess they could also provide some people with alibis if under suspicion...the uses are endless.'

'Yes, that's what Van Tam said from the very start, when I made it through the audition.'

'Well, what other positives are there...apart from deriving pleasure from capturing your dreams and daily pursuits?'

'I guess they could come in handy if there was another pandemic...what with them making a mess of the contact-tracing app during the COVID-19 crisis...able to tell exactly who came into contact with an infected person via the cameras...that's in addition to allowing someone to keep timeless memories without worrying about capturing photos or the like...plus they can choose which footage they want to retain using the new Eye-Spy editing suite software.'

'You'd see people acting strangely and doing slow head-sweeps in order for the cameras to pick up a certain view or to encompass their surroundings,' Troy said, managing a laugh and acting it out as he spoke.

'Or allow criminals to case a joint or observe people's daily habits without looking suspicious.'

'Well, from a health perspective; it would benefit those suffering with repeated nightmares to have visual logs for dream analysts to accurately study; to help them pinpoint the root cause and devise ways to help them as a result.'

'And we haven't even touched on the potential for companies to use the Dream Watcher as part of their interview process. Just imagine that…'we'd like to see your last three dreams before we decide on who gets the job'…able to obtain a much better impression of the person's character and replacing the need for psychometric testing.'

'Like Van Tam said; its uses are limitless; hence he's so desperate to ensure its release…even with the fatalities that have occurred since it's been under development.'

'Fatalities?' Troy responded quickly in a serious tone, his smile having now disappeared.

'Sorry, yeah…I didn't tell you…around two weeks ago, one of the Dreamers had a complete meltdown…attributed to the Dream Watcher and a weird phenomenon called a dream vortex; where a person starts to dream about the process of watching their dreams…and their brain can no longer decipher where the reality finishes and their imagination begins. It then continues to spiral out of control, affecting the person's autonomic nervous system, which then shuts down the vital functions of their body.'

Troy looked shocked.

'She was a good friend...her name was Lorna; I just wish I'd known about the potential risk before auditioning...I would never have entertained the idea otherwise...and if she'd known about it, then she'd still be alive today. I miss her so much.'

'I'm sorry Jared.'...

After a short pause, Jared continued.

'The good thing is I have many memories of her retained within my Dream Watcher from dreaming about her and also video I captured through the Eye-Spy lenses when we met up for social events outside of work.'

'So, can I see one of your dreams?' Troy asked, more curious now to see the results of the technology that Jared had explained.

Jared looked up, returning to the moment and focused on his friend across the room.

'Sure...I'll show you a dream I had just last night...it's only around five minutes long...it's pretty run of the mill but it'll give you an idea of what the technology can do.'

CHAPTER 18

After the pair climbed the stairs to the cinema room, Troy sat on one of the large footstools nearest to the projection wall. Jared switched on the peripherals at the back of the room housed on a glass unit, and after the menu appeared in front of them, beamed from the projector, he made his selection.

'Wow!' Troy exclaimed in surprise. He was impressed with the picture quality and amazed at the fact that he recognised certain places and objects that were personal to his friend, and which could therefore not have been made up by the system. It appeared the Dream Watcher could really do what Jared had claimed and he felt excited and unnerved in equal measure.

'I want to show you something else,' Jared exclaimed, now selecting a different dream from the home menu after the one they were watching had finished. It was something he'd been desperate to tell his friend about from the minute he saw him.

Within a few seconds the tropical oasis in the desert appeared; Troy gazing at the scene, captivated by the level of detail.

Jared walked over to the screen, with Troy curious as to his friend's sudden action.

'Watch this!' Jared announced, as he stood right up against the projection and slowly reached out both his arms towards it. After a few seconds he pulled his cupped hands, now filled with water from the spring, back out and splashed his friend in a jovial manner.

Troy's reaction was instant; falling back off the edge of the footstool onto the floor, touching the water on his face and scrabbling backwards to try and get further away. He was struggling to understand what he'd just witnessed; something Jared had very much anticipated.

As Troy lay in a state of shock, he watched Jared reach back into the image on the wall. After plucking a leaf from one of the plants in the foreground, he brought it into the room and held it up for Troy to see. Jared was used to the phenomenon by now and stood smiling at his friend.

Troy felt very uneasy as he lay perfectly still on the floor. He didn't know what to think, assuming there must be some sleight of hand involved to explain it, especially as Jared seemed so blasé about the whole situation.

After a few more seconds, Troy got up and walked towards his friend; reaching out to touch the leaf that had been inexplicably produced from the projected image. His eyes widened as he felt its coarse texture, and with water continuing to trickle down his face, he was visibly scared.

'So this is what Dreamex have created?' his measured response so quiet that it was almost inaudible.

'Not exactly,' Jared replied, having handed Troy the leaf as both sat down on opposite sofas. 'Their project was inventing the Dream Watcher; technology that could interpret your dreams, record them and enable playback like you've seen…which is mind-blowing enough, I realise…but being able to enter your own dream world was never something they discussed with me…I really don't think they're aware that this could happen. I haven't mentioned anything to Van

Tam; even though I get on well with him...but it doesn't get any weirder than this, Troy...imagine what we can do now!'

'We?'

'Yes; the reason I wanted you to see this is because I need to know if someone else can enter my dream, or if it's only the dreamer that can...I'm thinking of completely immersing myself in a dream...but the only thing stopping me trying was worrying about getting back. I can't be sure I'd be able to get back here from my dream world by myself...but if someone else could reach inside, then maybe they could pull me back out or indicate where I could find the exit...like a gateway or portal.'

'You mean you want me to try and do what you just did?'

'Yes, just give it a go...'

'Jared, you're talking to me as if this is normal...like you just asked me to come round to give you a hand shifting furniture...not spot for you whilst you entered your own dream; a dream that was recorded whilst you were asleep by a machine that you helped develop, and which you've now beamed onto your wall. This is hurting my brain so much...I could really do with a drink.'

'Just put your hand into the projection...it only has to be a little way, just so we know if it's possible.'

Troy looked at the desert scene on the wall, shutting his eyes for a moment, hoping it would somehow change his situation. Jared could see how hesitant his friend was to attempt it and so placed his hand on Troy's and slowly raised it towards the screen. Troy was acting as though he was being asked to put his hand in a fire, and very reluctant to do it.

'Just trust me...it won't hurt, I promise.'

Now under his own volition, Troy reached out further towards the image and this time he saw it; his hand disappearing slowly from the room and appearing seamlessly in Jared's dream, instantly feeling the heat of the desert climate and the light spray of the spring water. He quickly pulled his hand back out, relieved to see it was still intact and functioning as he purposely manipulated his fingers and thumb; he'd done it.

Realising this was proof that anyone could enter someone's dream world, Jared asked Troy to test the principle further and try plucking a leaf from the foliage nearest to him. Troy, however, was not ready for that and made his feelings known.

'Okay...let's leave it for now then...let you get your head around it...it took me a few days.'

There was a silence in the room as Jared started switching everything off; Troy sat very still, gazing down at his outstretched arm and at the moisture that covered it. He looked even more confused than before, contemplating what had just happened.

CHAPTER 19

'So why are you so determined to enter completely into one of your dreams?' Troy asked in a very concerned manner, after the pair started walking back down to the ground floor. 'It's surely too dangerous to contemplate.'

'Well this is going to sound even crazier, Troy, but I've had something playing on my mind ever since I realised I could enter my dreams. I have quite a few recorded dreams involving Lorna, and it dawned on me that if I could completely enter one of them…then perhaps I could save her and bring her back through the screen and into our reality…I did say it was crazy…but so is finding that you can put your arm into a dream world and pull out a leaf from a plant…It may be possible, so it's got to be worth a shot, right?'

Troy gave his friend a double-take and shook his head in bewilderment.

'I can kind of get my head around the principle of the Dream Watcher…but how is it even possible to be able to enter a 2D-screen and walk around in a new world?'

'I can't answer that one Troy…there is no science that can explain it…this goes beyond anything we thought possible…it's like we're already dreaming and will wake up at some point.'

'Well, have you come up with anything that makes sense of it…over the last few days?'

After reaching the kitchen and Cindy greeting them both, Troy took a seat at the breakfast bar, whilst Jared leant up against the kitchen top opposite, reflecting on what his friend had asked. ...

After a short pause he responded.

'It seems impossible that science can explain it...it's well outside the realms of physics as we know it...so I asked myself what would need to happen for this to work? Was thinking that perhaps the sensation we get when touching something is potentially only what our brain is telling us how it should feel...like we've been conditioned to believe that an object's physical characteristics are as they are and yet in reality nothing has a physicality; just a bunch of random patterns, colours and shapes that our brain interprets to us as solid and definable objects...

It's like light reflecting and refracting; shadows adding depth and interacting within the images we see all around us at the same time...we take it for granted; never questioning it despite how weird and wonderful it may appear...we just accept it as 'naturally occurring'. Have you ever thought how utterly bizarre it is to be able to see the depth of our own reality through a mirror? To see things within it and around corners that you couldn't see even if you turned around and looked that way yourself? ...

Everything we see in our day to day lives are things we've been conditioned to believe are the norm and it never crosses our mind to question any of it...that must be why we can enter the dream world as we've questioned the possibility of doing it...challenged the constraints of our mind that tell us how things are and work and by believing it, have opened up a new dimension that has always existed before...

I mean, have you ever woken up and felt weird; as though you're not really there in that place; at that time? It seems alien for a brief moment that you're actually present in a real-life world? It's happened to me on a few occasions in my life. Although I recognise my surroundings; it feels so surreal...the idea or reason why we're here on Earth seems too bizarre to comprehend; too bizarre for it to be really happening...as strange as it sounds I've then felt compelled to touch my arm; to convince myself that I'm real and that I'm really here; that there is a world of others that exist just like me outside the walls of my bedroom. How do we know we've been asleep for as long as we have and that we've been in the same place the entire night? We really only have our clock or the light to convince us but what if everyone was being affected at the same time and nobody could see it?'

'You're beginning to make it sound like an episode of the X-Files...you suggesting that people are being whisked off into alien spacecraft and used for testing purposes?'

'I realise it sounds like fantasy, Troy...but then this is unbelievable, right?' Maybe it turns out that the concept of everything co-existing is too difficult for us to comprehend...like the beginning of the universe and whether something can be created from nothing...if there was a big bang then why were the ingredients for the big-bang already in place? It couldn't just appear...

And then there's the reason why? What purpose do we have...just going from A to B over 70, 80 or 90 years and trying to elicit as much enjoyment from it as possible...if we're lucky? And why is it that some don't get a fair crack at it compared to others and through no fault of their own? The more I think about it the more I feel we're an experiment; like lab-rats scurrying around our own little environment being watched like animals in the cage. Having advanced brains enables us to question our own mortality...our position within the universe. No matter how close we may be in a relationship to others, though, we're only truly aware of our own consciousness, the only one we can truly understand, trust, communicate and reason with in order to come to the right decisions; even when we go to sleep at night.'

'Well, I can see you've definitely been giving this some thought, Jared. You've reminded me about something that happened in my youth. I was around nine or maybe ten-years-old at the time; I'd just seen Superman 2 and one part in particular was playing on my mind as I went to bed shortly after. I couldn't comprehend the idea of Zod, Ursa and Non floating out into space within the glass plane they'd been incarcerated in…for what would, in effect, be forever…it made me contemplate death, and at that age the concept upset me…

My mum told my brother to come into my bedroom to comfort me. He said he'd thought exactly the same about death at my age but it turned out years later that he'd made it all up just to make me feel better. The human mind is indeed a strange one when we have the tools to question ourselves, how we function and why we're here…and like Dreamex; having the intelligence to invent the science that can interpret our individual thoughts and even record them.'

'True…but as we make technological advances in visual entertainment and things are becoming so 'life-like'; then perhaps our preconditioned brains can no longer discriminate between the original parameters of the world we inhabit…and the parameters of our own newly-created fantasies, including the dreams I project onto the wall. As a result, we are able to walk through the screen as though it's part of our own reality; an overlap of two 3D-worlds where the space inside the dream morphs with our real world.

Others cannot see it as the gateway in and out is only through the projection on the wall.'

'Did you say you had some whisky? I could really do with a shot or two right now...hate the stuff usually but hey; I'm thinking I'll give it a go right now.'

'Well I really want to see if I can meet Lorna in one of my dreams and test my theory. It's one thing to interact with a static desert scene...but to be able to have a conversation with someone who has died and bring them back into our reality would be incredible. We've got to try. If we can pull it off then we'll have not only re-written history but completely turned the world as we know it on its head.'

Jared turned around, and after opening one of the cupboards in front of him, took out two whisky tumblers and a full bottle of single malt; pulling out the corked top and decanting two healthy measures, pushing one across the kitchen top towards Troy to help him take the edge off his nervous tension.

CHAPTER 20

'So run this idea by me again. You're going to try entering one of your dreams featuring Lorna and then see if you can lead her back into your cinema room and need me to help guide you back here?'

'That's the plan, yeah...I've experimented with some other dreams of mine and I've noticed that unless the scene is static, like the oasis in the desert; once my hand enters and the dream plays out on the screen, my arm completely disappears from view...it seems it remains in the dream world at the point where I inserted it as I continued to feel the same things I was already touching...it felt a little disconcerting to say the least...

That's why I'd need you to leave your arm in once you'd helped me to step in, as otherwise I wouldn't know where to find your hand inside the dream and my gateway back to the real world. The only other way you could get hold of me otherwise, is if I happened to be in the exact scene that was being shown on screen at that precise moment...which is unlikely to say the least...oh and pausing the screen didn't work when my hand was already immersed; I tried that too.'

'It's one thing to bring a leaf from the dream world...but a person? That's rather a big step up wouldn't you say? And if you manage to bring her into our reality, then what about the potential knock-on effects to everything that has happened since?'

'I've thought about that...but I'm confident that Lorna's life did not massively influence the world around her...to the extent that bringing her back would cause too much of a detrimental effect on anything…and besides, I'm sure her family and friends would love to see her again.'

'But that in itself would cause unforeseen ripples throughout other people's lives, right? They surely wouldn't be able to cope with her reappearance…especially the people who saw her at the funeral home and watched her being buried.'

'Well, we don't even know if it's possible…it's going to be an experiment and one that I hope will work…people are alive in dreams, Troy, I know it…you just have to believe it.'

'You're suggesting that nobody really dies, then? This is completely beyond me, Jared.'

'Perhaps nobody does…they just continue to live on in a different reality…and when you see them again in your dreams, it's not your subconscious that's making them appear at all…maybe it's not happening by chance, but because they've entered your dream world whilst you're asleep… come to say hello and make sure you're okay…it's the best time to do it as people are usually too busy during the day…although they can still send signals that remind you of them in all kinds of ways…

I remember when I was sitting at my desk at the Bank one day and a beautiful bird hovered up against the window right next to me…there was nobody else around, despite being an open-plan office and it stayed there for what seemed like an age…probably only a few seconds or so in reality…but It'd never happened before or since…I knew it was the anniversary of my Nan's passing that day as I never forget a date…but it was only later that I realised the two must have been connected…I believe it was her coming to say hello and letting me know she was okay…

The same when my brother died. My mum and dad would see black butterflies appearing randomly at different times afterwards, having never seen them before...his name was Nigel, deriving from Latin and meaning black...

There was another occasion that happened to me a few weeks after he died, which was the year after my Nan passed away; the loss of my brother still very raw and in my thoughts daily. Two geese flew from around the side of my house as I stood in the back yard and not more than eight feet directly above my head, both honking in unison, before veering straight up and high into the sky...I watched them disappear from sight and it made me think immediately that it was my Nan and brother reunited...

Surely these things couldn't all have been coincidences? Instead, I believe those leaving us are able to affect our reality still...we can't just ask them to send us a sign on demand, though...it's much more difficult for it to be done, as it has to fit within the parameters of our world. It has to be something that if anyone else saw it, they would not question or interpret it as anything other than a normal aspect of the reality that they've been conditioned to accept.'

'So, you think someone who dies has the ability to communicate with us in some way...and we just have to look out for the signs?'

'Perhaps they can choose to watch us, as we are in a dream world to them...the Dream Watcher just provided me with a reason to believe. It's maybe why people with a greater belief have developed the use of those parts of their brain that we are told usually lie dormant...and why they have premonitions or psychic abilities, as they interact with those from their dream world...those who have already seen things and can pass the information on...it's perhaps why some escape death or find fortune...maybe it's not luck at all...but because they've been told and chose to listen…perhaps there's no such thing as fate…

I mean, have you ever tried to clear your mind of everything…trying to reach a state of pure relaxation as you lay there in bed before trying to sleep? It's impossible to do as you're then thinking about the act itself…your brain cannot help but select random thoughts….almost like it has a mind of its own and you're not fully in control of it…like a memory lottery…opening a dictionary and pointing randomly at a word on a page…there is no way of knowing what will be brought into your waking conscience…and most of the time it's so unrelated to the moment or of recent events that it seems crazy why it did…

Perhaps something or someone else caused it to come to the surface…because they wanted you to remember it…perhaps the key is to work out why…that random thought can then shape how you think of other things closely related to it and in some cases it can actually affect your short-term outlook…maybe prompting you to do something different the next day….these are memories that would otherwise lay undiscovered…locked away to be never woken again…just imagine how many memories that we never think about again in our lifetimes…'…

There was a long pause as Troy remained transfixed, trying to interpret everything his friend had said.

'Well if you truly believe it's possible we can bring someone from your dream world back into this reality; don't you think we should test the theory on something smaller first? Perhaps a live animal…just to see what happens?'

'You're probably right, Troy. I'm just desperate to save Lorna and see her again…I've never felt so impatient, but I guess as long I have the dreams saved, I can revisit them whenever, and there isn't a need to rush into it...I'll have to scan through my previous dreams and see what I can find...there was one I had not long ago where a dog was barking at me...not a ferocious dog...just a family pet...I remembered why it had featured in my dream after watching it, as it was the same breed that had caused me to jump a little after barking at me when exiting a shop earlier that day, when the owner had tied it up outside and it had begun to rain. I think that was a week or so ago.'

'But I thought you hated dogs?'

'Hate is a bit strong...I don't hate them...guess I just like things clean and tidy, and realise you'd have to forgo all that if you had one...or be constantly cleaning up after it.'

Troy leant his head right back whilst downing the remainder of his whisky, grimacing from its effects for a brief moment, before placing the tumbler down on the breakfast bar.

'Well, I need to go and meet my sister. I said I'd babysit for her. Just let me know how you get on...doesn't matter what time...I'm curious to know whether it can be done...to bring something living from your dream into our world.'

Troy closed his eyes briefly, pressing his fingers and thumb into the bridge of his nose and remained perfectly still; the disbelief at how ridiculous his last sentence sounded hitting home, before breaking into a smile of delirium, now shaking his head.

'You'll be the second person to know. Thanks for your help and for not running away from this...I really appreciate it.'

'You're more than welcome,' Troy replied smiling, the nonsensical phrase having provided them both with a laugh in the past and the reason they continued to use it.

Jared saw his friend out and waved him off, before closing the front door, and making his way enthusiastically up both sets of stairs to the cinema room to check through his previous dreams.

Chapter 21

The next evening, Troy made his way over to Jared's, buoyed by his friend's excited appearance on the holophone message that he'd picked up during work.

After ascending the stairs together, Troy opened the door to the cinema room off the small landing. He was surprised to find a veritable stash of random furniture and equipment piled up in one of the corners under the sloping ceiling, akin to the storeroom of an antiques emporium; also noticing that some of it was identical to that already in situ in Jared's house, and even a duplicate of a table in the same room.

'You brought all this out of your dreams?' Troy exclaimed rummaging through the bric-a-brac.

'Yes, I needed to see if I could…and then realised I could do with some replacements. I couldn't find another table like this anywhere and that one hasn't got a crack on one of its legs,' Jared replied, laughing.

Noticing that everything Jared had brought back could only be classed as inanimate, Troy looked puzzled and turning to his friend, asked, 'So, did you manage to bring anything 'living' back through the screen?'

At that exact moment, there was the sound of scratching from the other side of the door. Troy instinctively turned to look towards it before quickly reverting his gaze back to Jared, with an inquisitive expression on his face. Jared beamed at his friend and walked over to open it.

'There's someone I'd like you to meet.'

A Highland Terrier ran into the room and started making a fuss of Troy before jumping onto the sofa nearest to Jared.

'This is Sprocket.'

'Wow! So it actually works then,' Troy said; overcome with surprise as he reached out to touch the dog to make sure it was real.

'Yes, although I don't know what the real Sprocket is going to make of it if we bump into him at the shop or out walking.'

Both Troy and Jared laughed at the concept; it was a really difficult one to get their heads around but with the dogs unable to speak, there would be no chance of them giving the game away.

'So, I guess this means…'

Troy started to speak when Jared cut him off.

'Yes, there's a good chance it will also work with Lorna. I found a perfect dream we can use too…I was up all night trying to select the best one,' he said, smiling and raising his eyebrows.

'Well, after I left here last night, I couldn't stop thinking about everything…my head was buzzing and I couldn't really sleep as a result. If 'you' can enter a dream and alter reality in some way, then wouldn't that make it possible to change other things that happened in the past?'

'As long as someone had dreamt about it, then I guess the same principles would exist.'

'Wow! There'd be so much we could put right, if that's true...we could help so many people with the benefit of hindsight...we could point out to the engineers that using iron rivets for the hull of titanic wasn't safe, or go and pick up the shrapnel off the runway at Charles De Gaul airport that started the chain of events that downed Concorde... or prevent the terrorists from gaining access to the flights during 911. I know there are bigger things that happened in the past but I'm just thinking of examples...and I guess there'd be a cut-off point as to which scenarios we could enter. It would depend on someone dreaming about the event...like something that took place during World War Two.'

'Well, I think we might be getting way ahead of ourselves...but I guess so, in theory...but like you said...someone would have to dream about the events first and that would mean recalling them vividly. The person would have to have a decent knowledge of the event in order to provide the necessary level of detail...and even then, if the objects weren't present in the Dream Vault, then the system may not be able to interpret them at all.'

'There'd be no such thing as regrets any more if you could go back and change the things you weren't happy about...especially as it's those occurrences that continue to play on your mind. Anything etched in your short term memory would be more likely to appear in your dreams, right? We all make mistakes which we would like to erase; now we may have the chance to do that...'

'Like I said, Troy...we don't even know if changing something in a dream will alter anything in reality. If it does, then that opens up endless possibilities of changing other things in history for the better, like you mentioned. We need to be very wary and must consider how anything we change could affect our current reality; things may get worse instead and there's no real way of us knowing exactly. Let's see what happens when we try to save Lorna.'

'Well, when did you want to try?'

'Are you in a rush to get somewhere tonight?' Jared replied, tipping his head and raising an eyebrow.

'Okay, let's do it,' Troy exclaimed reluctantly before carrying out an exaggerated swallow, and Jared noticed his eyes looked full of trepidation.

After knocking back another shot of single malt to steady their nerves, the pair agreed it was time to traverse the stairs once again, shutting Sprocket in the kitchen first to prevent him from jumping back through into the dream world.

Jared had already found the particular dream he knew featured Lorna and set it up to play, the beginning now projected onto the wall.

'Don't let go of my hand until I know everything is alright on the other side!' Jared explained clearly to Troy who was positioned right next to the screen, with his hand out ready.

'Hey, what happens if I get pulled in by you or someone else with my arm dangling in there?' Troy suddenly exclaimed realising the possibility.

'Here, tie this cord around your leg and the coffee table…its solid oak and probably weighs the same as you,' Jared replied passing him an obsolete extension cable he still had in storage in one of the footstools.

After tying the lead to the table, Troy was much happier; unable to move the coffee table by pulling his leg away from it and relieved he'd realised before Jared would potentially leave him on his own in the room.

The pair then carried out some random breathing exercises, with Jared even slapping himself in the face to try to enact an increased alertness. They were both ready.

Troy wished Jared good luck and gave him a reassuring smile.

'Just remember not to let go of my hand…I'll tap you three times like this…meaning you can let go, right?'

'Right…three times…got you.'

Troy adopted a stance like he was at the starting line of a long distance race; legs spread and with one foot pushed against the wall underneath the projected image. He took hold of Jared's left hand with his right hand.

'Ready?' Jared asked in a serious tone.

Troy nodded, whilst staring straight at Jared, the pair not knowing what was going to happen. The screen showed the entrance to Dreamex headquarters. Jared lifted his right leg and slowly moved it forwards into the image on the wall. He found a slight drop on the other side before tentatively bringing his foot down onto a firm surface. It was now time to step completely into his dream…

CHAPTER 22

Troy readied himself to pull his friend back at any sign of complications. Jared moved his head closer to the screen. It would be the biggest test yet and by far the greatest indicator of how the two worlds co-existed, losing contact with Troy and the security of his own reality, whilst transported into the realms of his own imagination.

As Jared's face began to penetrate the boundary, the light became very bright causing him to close his eyes immediately and keep them tightly shut. There had been no resistance or noticeable changes when putting his hand in previously, but this was different; feeling strange sensations as his head made the transition. Jared could still see how bright the light was even through his eyelids and felt his face rippling as though enclosed in a high g-force centrifuge; his breathing also affected.

Fortunately, the experience only lasted for a few seconds. Opening his eyes slowly, he could see the steps up to the entrance of the Dreamex headquarters and felt a little cold; the temperature being much lower than that of his cinema room and he wished he had put on another layer. He could both see and feel Troy's hand still holding onto his, seemingly floating in front of him; a very bizarre sight with nothing else around it other than the dream world which he was now fully immersed in.

Jared tapped Troy's hand three times as per the instruction; Troy released his grip giving a thumbs-up gesture, hopeful that Jared would still be able to see it. Jared smiled briefly, realising that he was now on his own in a world where he had no idea if things would be the same as he was used to, and that made him very wary.

Suddenly, Troy's hand disappeared from sight and Jared started to panic, like an astronaut on a spacewalk realising their tether had been cut and there was no way of getting back to the ship. Seconds later, to his indescribable relief, Troy's hand reappeared, although further away from him. Jared was just glad to see it.

In the time it took Troy to replace his hand into the dream, the video being shown through the projector had moved on a little and was why his arm was now in a different position relative to him. The reason Troy had removed his arm may have been a trivial one, but the moment had affected Jared greatly and he took some deep breaths to calm himself. He was now keen to forge on to find Lorna as soon as he could and bring her back to his friend's outstretched arm.

Troy remained motionless by the projection screen. Ten minutes had passed since he'd seen Jared. He was having difficulty keeping his arm outstretched and had taken to using his other to prop it up.

He felt paranoid, too. The prospect of someone or something dragging him into the dream was one that he dwelt on as he was unable to see his own arm within the image and what was happening around it. He was reminded of the scene from Flash Gordon where Flash and Barin were commanded to place their hands into holes in a tree stump and hope that the wood beast would not sting them to death.

Just as his mind began to wander, Troy felt something suddenly touch his hand and the shock caused a reflex reaction making him pull his arm away from the perceived threat. But the grip on the other side was strong enough to keep it there, and Troy's terror calmed after feeling the three taps and realising who it was.

Gripping with his hand, Troy began pulling the person on the other side towards him into the cinema room and was relieved to see Jared's hand and lower arm emerge through the screen. Troy closed his eyes temporarily. His relief was palpable; their plan had worked and his friend would not be stuck in his dream world.

As Jared's face began to appear, Troy could see that his friend was smiling, suggesting that his mission had been a success.

'I've found her Troy…I explained everything to her as quickly as I could…she's holding my other hand…pull me out and I'll bring Lorna out too.'

Troy continued to pull his friend into the room until only Jared's other hand was out of sight. Letting go of his friend, Jared then continued to bring Lorna in by himself. However, as soon as Lorna's hand broke the screen between the two realities, both Troy and Jared made a shocking discovery. Jared felt Lorna's grip slacken suddenly and they both noticed that her hand and arm had decomposed; her carpal and metacarpal bones visible.

Jared released his grip on Lorna's skeletal hand immediately and fell backwards onto the floor breathing hard. It was obvious what happened caused adrenaline to course through his veins and enact his flight response. Jared and Troy watched as Lorna's hand slipped swiftly back into the screen and out of sight.

'What the fuck?' Troy exclaimed having moved away in horror to the opposite side of the coffee table, his leg still shackled to it. The room then fell silent, only the faint hum of the projector could be heard. It was not supposed to happen that way; the pair both visibly affected by what they'd just seen.

After a few minutes they regained their composure, Jared released Troy's leg from the cord and switched off the equipment before the pair went downstairs to the kitchen. Without uttering a single word to each other, Jared took out the whisky from the cupboard, which was now only two-thirds full, and poured out two large measures, passing Troy one. Sprocket was pleased to see them both and ran between the pair, jumping up at them, his tail wagging enthusiastically. Taking a couple of large gulps, Jared then began trying to rationalise what they had both witnessed.

'Lorna was alive and well in my dream…she even recognised me, Troy…I spoke to her, touched her and explained what had happened and why I was there…of course she was sceptical and thought I was mad but when I brought her out of Dreamex and into the car park and she saw your arm floating in space…that's when she believed me. I told her I was there to save her life…she put her trust in me.'

'So what happened…why didn't it work like it did with the dog?'

'It must be because she's already dead…in this reality.'

'So you're saying because Lorna is already dead in our reality, then there's no way she can be brought here…She's only alive in dreams?'

'It seems that way Troy…that must be why her body was dead and decaying when she entered the room.'

'So there's no way we can save her then and bring her back into our world?'

'I think we're going to have to get hold of Lorna's dreams and enter one of them instead. We need to ascertain what caused her to lose her last job and reverse it...I've had a long time to think about it since she died...if she hadn't lost her last job, then she wouldn't have needed to audition at Dreamex, right? If we can change something that happened to her via her dreams, then maybe it will alter our reality and she'll still be alive.'

'You mean like time travel?'

'No, not based on time but of the mechanics of her dream imagination...her subconscious thoughts...change those and it may alter the reality around her that caused her to have those dreams in the first place.'

'But surely we'd need to see her dreams from before she started at Dreamex.'

'Not necessarily. That's the beauty of dreams...even though she started work at Dreamex when I did, that doesn't mean she hadn't dreamt about her past since...maybe some bad memories that won't go away...her friend Chloe intimated that she had gone through a very rough time before Dreamex and that's why she quit her last job, but that's all Lorna told her apparently and didn't go into specifics...if we can potentially locate the reason for her going through the 'bad patch' then maybe we can do something about it and ensure she remains in her job.'

'Well how are you going to get hold of Lorna's dreams?'

'Well what do we know? We know that all Dreamers have provided Dreamex with their Dream Cards since starting, which retains a person's dreams over a maximum of around two hours or around a week's worth on average for me...the data is then uploaded onto the Super Computer at Dreamex headquarters and it's there that the data miners then use this to develop what they call the Dream Vault. If I can gain access to the Super Computer, then I should be able to download Lorna's dreams and then bring them up via the projector, just like mine...'

'Okay...so that sounds good in theory...you can do that, right?'

'It's not going to be easy, though...the only people who have access to the room which houses the Super Computer are two senior data scientists...known as the Gatekeepers, and Van Tam himself...'

'But you get on well with Van Tam...you said he confides in you a lot...'

'Get on with him maybe, but he's not going to let me take dream data for my own benefit and without asking why...'

'Well, I know this is going to sound crazy, but can't you just enter one of your dreams and enter the Super Computer room and download the data from there and then get back here like you just did?'

'I've never seen the Super Computer though, Troy...it's housed in the basement in an extremely secure part of the building and where access is restricted...so consequently I've never dreamt about it...without having actually seen it then I'll only have my own interpretation of what it may look like, and that won't be good enough to enable me to copy the dream data...

I would have to enter the dreams of one of the Gatekeepers or Van Tam himself...that would mean having to visit their home addresses and stealing information from their Dream Watcher or Dream Cards...which would be very risky indeed...especially if I was caught during the act...and It's unlikely we're going to locate a dream of Van Tam's including the Super Computer.'

'Well, what are we going to do then? It sounds like neither of those options is viable.'

'I'm going to have to see if I can gain access to the Super Computer room...I think that's my best shot out of the two, but it's still not going to be easy.'

'How about using your cameras in your contact lenses to do a recce down in the basement where the Super Computer is based? It'll give you something to work off and plan what you need to do to access it, especially if you can watch one of these Gatekeepers entering...'

'I like your thinking Troy...but that would still mean me having to gain access to the basement...another drawback is that Dreamex have sensors in place to detect if anyone is wearing the Eye-Spy lenses on entry...it's to stop any information from inside the building being leaked into the public domain or to other tech companies, who'd be willing to pay a handsome sum for it...I'll have to sleep on it and work out what to do...the fact that everyone trusts me there, including security, may just be my golden ticket and allow me to get away with it...'

Chapter 23

The next evening Troy received a call from an excited Jared, whilst on his way home from work, via his in-car holophone.

'I remembered something last night, Troy. There is someone who wears their lenses at Dreamex and for whom the rules don't apply...Van Tam himself...I need to access his Eye-Spy lens feed when I know he's visiting the Super Computer...he goes down there at least a couple of times each day.'

'So how will you go about getting hold of that...did you say the feed is sent remotely to someone's Dream Watcher...meaning we'd still have to find a way into his house without alerting anyone?'

'Like I said, gaining access to the house and being able to get hold of his Dream Watcher, or substitute it for another unit would be too risky, Troy. The information is sent remotely to his Dream Watcher, yes, but the lens camera feed also runs through the Eye-Spy software programme, which can be held on any supporting device. Van Tam has it on his computer in his office as I've seen the icon above his desk on the holograph-display...I'll need to open it up when I know he's on his way down to the Super Computer and capture the information somehow...

He sometimes asks me to do things for him from his desk, so my presence there shouldn't arouse too much suspicion from the other execs, but it's vital I'm not spotted keeping a track on Van Tam for obvious reasons.'

'Well, when were you thinking of trying to do it?'

'I'm going to do it tomorrow before the weekend, as it'll give us time to go over what I've seen and allow us to plan for next week and obtaining Lorna's data from the Super Computer...besides, I'm too impatient...I'm no good at waiting...just want to get on with it.'

'So how are you going to capture the data from Van Tam down in the basement?'

'Well I think it best not to record it on any hardware...if I get searched then they'd find it and I'd be in all sorts of trouble, not to mention it would put an end to what we're trying to achieve.'

'So how are you going to get around that then?'

'If it's okay with you, Troy, I was thinking it would be best if I relayed the information directly to you over the holophone in Van Tams' office...you'll have to write it all down accurately so we have notes on what I need to do...access to doors and any codes I'll need to input...as well as looking out for where I'm likely to be confronted by any Dreamex staff down there...will you be able to take a call from me at work?'

'Shouldn't be a problem...my boss is away and I can always say it's a personal matter anyway.'

'Great! Well, he usually goes down to the basement as part of his rounds first thing, around nine and then again just before noon...so you'll need to be available then.'

'No problem...good luck Jared!'

Troy signed off with an army-style salute to his friend before both their images disappeared. Their call having ended, Jared climbed the stairs to his room, having just arrived home from his day at work, dropping his bag down next to the bed and placing his jacket over one of the posts of its metallic frame. He then sat at his piano and stared across at his bedroom window, the curtains always drawn and a single work-shirt hung from the curtain pole on a hanger, an instant visual reminder of which day of the week it was, the four other hangers now redundant, balanced perfectly in a vertical line next to it.

Jared was systematically running through what he needed to do; now contemplating whether or not the whole idea was viable, and if the prospect of trying to carry it off was worth the risk. However, nothing else mattered more than trying to save Lorna in his mind, and that realisation led to an instant change in his mood, especially having interacted with her in his dream. An involuntary smile emerged and he felt a sudden appetite to play something uplifting and positive, his fingers creating the dulcet tones of the opening bars of Johann Strauss's Blue Danube Waltz as he lost himself in the realms of the timeless piece.

Chapter 24

After arriving at the Dreamex headquarters the next day, Jared made his way to the staff restaurant for breakfast. He was not feeling very hungry at all; his anxiety levels higher than usual given he'd been mulling over the things that could go wrong with his plan. Breaking his boss' trust would not go down very well with him at all if caught, and the act of spying on him through his own eyes was something highly immoral. However, Jared realised he would potentially arouse suspicion if he deviated from his usual routine, and that was the last thing he wanted to do on today of all days.

Logging into his computer at his desk, Jared pretended to look busy; his seating position behind his desk gave him a great vantage point, witnessing all the comings and goings along the main corridor, which was flanked by the executive's offices, with Van Tam's directly opposite. He was even able to see someone about to exit his boss' room, given he could see the outline of their lower legs through the ventilation grilles mounted in both doors.

As per Van Tam's customary routine, it wasn't long before Jared noticed him about to leave on his daily rounds. He knew that would include a trip past the tech labs to check on any further progress made with finalising the Dream Watcher consoles before heading down to the Super Computer. After acknowledging Jared with a raised hand as he exited his office, Van Tam stopped briefly with another of the executive team in the corridor, before disappearing out of sight and off towards the main lifts.

Jared realised it was time. He picked up his tablet and some paperwork, to give the impression he had a purpose for making his way to Van Tam's office, gesticulating to those in the adjoining offices who noticed him walk past. He would usually stop to chat to some of them, but he didn't have time today; it was imperative he could see Van Tam's route down to the Super Computer.

Entering Van Tam's office, Jared closed the door until it was almost shut, leaving a small gap before placing the bits and pieces down on the desk. Sitting in the impressive seat, he located the computer hard drive and pressed the standby button for the holographic display, which appeared instantly; the image rising a couple of feet up from the desktop and displaying the different programmes and files that his boss had recently been working on.

Hearing some activity in the corridor outside, Jared paused briefly to scatter some of the paperwork across the desk to make him appear to be working as normal. Waiting for the noise to pass, he then scrolled down the holographic avatars until he located the Eye-Spy programme and selected the 3D symbol by reaching out his index finger and penetrating the slowly rotating image in front of him.

The display now showed a number of thumbnail screens within the options bar and one of them was Van Tam's own live feed through his lens cameras, although too small to elicit any real detail. He quickly increased the size of the image using both hands simultaneously to stretch the image out along both vertical and horizontal axis. Jared was now faced with a much clearer view and he was a lot happier with the result.

Thankfully for Jared, it appeared Van Tam had not yet made his way down to the basement; able to discern immediately that he was up on the fourth floor and carrying out a recce of the Dreamers test-labs. He would do this to ensure all Dreamers had arrived for work and all had their Dream Cards present from the previous night. The process had been the same every day for years. The lead scientists would populate all of the Dream Card data onto a larger version, which was then passed to either Van Tam or one of the two Gatekeepers, if he was otherwise engaged or away from the office, although an extremely rare event in itself.

With Van Tam the only one that would question what he was doing in his office, it was therefore handy that Jared could see exactly where he was at all times, always a step ahead and guaranteeing himself time to exit prior to his boss' arrival back in the Executive wing of the Dreamex headquarters.

As Jared followed Van Tam's route with interest, he watched as he came back down to the ground floor. It was at that point that he selected Troy's contact details on the holophone and after a short pause, Troy's image appeared to the side of the holographic computer display. There was no time for any conversation. Jared gave a running commentary and Troy recorded what his friend was saying to him.

Having been speaking for approximately eight minutes, Jared then witnessed Van Tam entering the stand-alone lift down to the basement and after emerging he plugged the master Dream Card into the wall of the Super Computer. However, just at that point, Jared was suddenly panicked to hear someone heading towards Van Tam's office, quickly changing the display and knocking out the holophone connection with Troy.

The door to the office opened after a polite knock and Jared recognised it was one of the Gatekeepers, wearing a technician's coat of brilliant white and with one arm of his spectacles resting on his bottom lip as he held them, appearing to be considering something. Jared was just a little flustered, suffering minor heart palpitations but tried to portray a calm and confident exterior.

'What has Alex got you doing for him this time?' he asked not looking shocked in the slightest to find Jared sat there.

'Just needed to finish something off from earlier in the week…didn't realise I hadn't completed it so was keen to get it out of the way before the weekend.'

'Do you know where he is, then?'

'He must be doing his rounds judging by the time.'

With that the older man nodded his head to acknowledge Jared's response and left the room.

Blowing out his cheeks, Jared returned to the previous display immediately, Van Tam's live feed appearing once again in front of him. However, as the image sprung up from the desk, Jared was in for a shock; his boss was now just around the corner and about to enter the executive corridor. There was no time for Jared to make an exit.

'You going to be long, Jared? I need to contact one of our clients…like ten minutes ago,' Van Tam exclaimed as he pushed open his office door and found Jared sat at his desk.

'Just finishing off those risk assessments you asked me to do…the ones you brought in to check if any of the other Dreamers were presenting cerebral signs that would indicate a greater potentiality for them experiencing a Dream Vortex in the future. Diane and Wendy weren't showing up on the portal as having been signed off, so I needed to replicate their data within the system and correlate it with the dates when I initially carried them out…just finished…here, you can have your seat back.'

Jared switched off the display and began collecting his paperwork together.

'None of them found out the real reason, right?'

'Well, I never mentioned anything whatsoever…I explained to them that you were just covering your back and that it was all part of the new health and safety policy.'

'Great! Good job Jared…as ever,' Van Tam exclaimed having now sat in his chair and watched as Jared looked back at him from the doorway with a somewhat forced and uncomfortable smile, before pulling the door closed.

CHAPTER 25

That evening, as Jared was returning from work, he saw someone he hadn't seen in a long time. It was the girl from the bus stop; the girl he'd fantasised about whilst he worked at the Bank. It had been years since he'd last seen her and was instantly reminded of the embarrassment that had prevailed following his attempt at setting up a date with her, causing him to laugh out loud. He hadn't even learnt her name. She was still a very beautiful girl and he had to concede that he'd certainly been somewhat optimistic expecting her to be interested in him.

Having been reminded of his past, Jared arrived home not long after to find Troy waiting for him. The pair set themselves up in the lounge so that Jared could view what Troy had recorded on his holophone, his explanation of the route and processes involved with Van Tam's access to the Super Computer.

'It's clear that Van Tam needed to bypass a biometric scanner to gain access to the part of the building where the lift down to the basement is housed,' Jared explained, the matter having played on his mind.

'So how are you going to get through that, if it's restricted?'

'Well everyone at Dreamex is designated with a different access level for the building…so my biometrics will only open the doors that I've been given permission…the security team handle all access issues, whether setting up new members of staff or updating privileges, which they do remotely from their office.'

'Are you saying you'll need to update your own access levels without them knowing?'

'No...that's far too difficult to consider...I have another idea to hopefully get around the problem.'

'And that is?' ...

There was a short pause before Jared replied.

'You know I said I get on well with almost everyone at Dreamex? Well, that includes the security team...I reckon if I can come up with a feasible story for why I need access to the tech labs downstairs, then there's one of them who may just help me out, especially as I know he hates Van Tam. If I can tailor my story to make out that he'll rollock me if I don't get a piece of work done for him, that requires the access, then I'm confident he'll side with me and help me out...he's also asked me if I can teach his daughter piano...so that's something else that might help sway his decision.'

'Are you sure he hates him that much?'

'He mentioned that Van Tam had issued him with a verbal warning after catching him flirting with colleagues in the staff restaurant...he didn't like that one bit as he reckoned he was only being friendly...so it's safe to say Van Tam is not on his Christmas card list.'

'Well, as long as you're sure you can trust him not to say anything.'

'I'm sure, don't worry...I've known him since I joined Dreamex...he cares very little for authority.'

'Right...sorry...I've just finished reading a book called 'No One Left to Trust' and it would appear I'm now more suspicious about everyone and everything than I thought possible,' Troy exclaimed forcing a grimace as though to accentuate his point.

'Apart from the biometric scanner, then the only other thing I'll need to negotiate is accessing the Super Computer room itself. It seemed that Van Tam only had to punch in a code on the display panel outside the lift as I saw him using the buttons...so that should be fine as long as I ensure to select them in the correct order.'

'And what then? Do you know how you're going to go about downloading Lorna's dream data?'

'I'm not too bad with tech so should be able to work it out easy enough...the biggest task will be managing to access the room...I'm going to take my Dream Watcher with me...it's the only thing I can think of with enough memory to enable me to download enough of Lorna's dreams to give us a realistic chance of seeing something that will explain why she left her last job and why she ended up having to audition for Dreamex...I can save my own dreams elsewhere so as not to lose them...'

'Well, I guess if you're found with a Dream Watcher on you, then it shouldn't look too out of place either.'

'Exactly! Plus Van Tam mentioned they would soon be providing us with the new prototype, the same one that would be available to the general public in the run up to Christmas.'

'So when are you going to try to gain access to the Super Computer?'

'It's going to have to be late one evening as Van Tam is always there until around six, six-thirty...but I'm going to have to make sure that Bill, the security guy, is on shift too, as I need him to provide me with access, remember? I can check out the rotas and see when he's in.'

'Right, well, is there anything else that you need to do as part of the plan?'

'If we manage to locate a dream of Lorna's that represents some kind of nightmare or reason why she went through a bad time in the past, when she lost her previous job, and prevent it from happening, the effect, theoretically, would mean she should reappear in this reality as though she'd never been away...still in her previous job. In order to check if it really worked, though, then we'd need to know where she lived...so I uplifted her address details whilst in Van Tam's office...that way we can check if she's still living there. It would be too late afterwards as her records would disappear from the files at Dreamex HQ as she would never have ended up working there.'

'Blimey, Jared...you really need to take it easy this weekend and give that brain of yours a rest,' Troy said now making his way to the front door.

'Yeah, I know...am planning to just chill this weekend; maybe create some new dreams.'

Troy shook his head whilst smirking back at his friend; Jared now laughing at his response. Troy then left the house and drove back home, leaving Jared to try to enjoy his weekend and prepare himself for D-Day.

Chapter 26

*'Come with me and you'll be
In a world of your imagination
Take a look and you'll see
Into your imagination
You'll begin with a spin
Travelling in the world of your creation
What you'll see will defy your explanation'*...

The music played from the speakers of the built-in TV set in one of the kitchen cupboards as Jared made a coffee; his eyes fixed to the Dreamex advert as it ran its course; trying to adjust his tie in between taking bites from his toast and creating a metallic backing-track from his over-stirring throughout.

Having let Sprocket, his West Highland Terrier, in from the back, he'd already decanted some biscuits into his bowl and made sure to top up the water next to it, patting him on the head as he guzzled them down, not stopping to take a breath.

'You're going to be late Jared, and I think I'd wear a coat if I were you; it's only 10 degrees Celsius out there,' came Cindy's voice, who's face now appeared on the same TV-unit, having automatically paused the current VT briefly to advise him. Quickly peering over at the clock on the wall, he sipped another mouthful of hot coffee and picked up the remaining piece of toast before rushing to the front door and grabbing his jacket from the rack in the hallway. He ensured he had his own Dream Watcher in his bag, from which he'd wiped the memory the previous night, after transferring the data.

'Don't mention it,' Cindy hollered rolling her eyes, the system detecting that Jared had left the house without any response and something that it had been well used to by now.

Jared spent his 20-minute commute checking the car's drop-down 14-inch entertainment display; having received a message from Cindy wishing him a good day at work and an update on what groceries and other household supplies he was running low on.

After exiting the shuttle-lane and steering the final few hundred yards, Jared could see it; the familiar and futuristic looking Dreamex Corporation building towering above the other companies, its silver window-surrounds glistening.

Parking up in his usual space, he got out of his car and walked briskly to the entrance steps, noting he only had three minutes to get in and up to the top floor where he was joining the other Dreamers for a meeting with Van Tam.

Van Tam always liked to start off the week with a catch-up, confirming progress made and whether the company was on track for its intended release date, the Dream Vault imperative to its success. It was also a chance for him to ensure the Dreamers felt very much part of the project and that morale remained high, especially given the relatively recent events surrounding Lorna, a well-liked and integral member of the team.

Following his final words, the room began emptying out and Jared made his way up the stairs to the exit. Waiting to get into one of the lifts back down to the first floor, he heard his name being called. Turning his head, he could see Van Tam walking with purpose towards him and the pair got into the lift together with the tail-end of the Dreamers. Having waited for the others to exit on the floor below, Van Tam began speaking to Jared, whilst they continued their descent.

'Sorry Jared...just wanted to ask how you were.'

'Hello Alex. You know me...living the dream,' he replied, the answer possibly the most repeated saying in the building and the slogan used by Dreamex on all its livery, stationery and advertising. It was also a catchphrase Van Tam tried to crowbar into conversation whenever he could, especially since Jared had been promoted to his position within the executive offices alongside him.

'Conscious it's been a few weeks since the awful business with Lorna. How are you bearing up? I know how much it's affected you...noticed you haven't seemed yourself since she died...and the data miners mentioned your dream frequency and productivity has been much lower than usual...are you sure you're getting enough sleep?'

Jared was a little spooked by Van Tam's timing; his concerns coming only a few days since he'd accessed his Eye-Spy lens feed and Lorna's personal details. He knew he needed to act normal and not give anything away.

Confirming to his boss that everything was fine and that he just wanted to make sure he was doing everything he could to assist the project, Van Tam grinned at Jared, whilst patting him on the back several times.

'That's great Jared...you're one of the shining lights around here and your enthusiasm and positive energy rubs off on the others...don't think I haven't noticed that...so I need you back in the saddle as soon as possible...have a good day,' and with that Van Tam disappeared into his office, leaving Jared reflecting on the timing once again.

CHAPTER 27

Later that evening, when almost all staff, including Van Tam, had left for home, Jared knew it was time to put the plan into operation. Placing his bag over his shoulder with his Dream Watcher inside, he left his office for the day, walking along the corridor and down the flight of stairs to the entrance foyer. He knew he would need to walk past the security desk en route and it was here that he'd seen Bill earlier in the day; the security officer he hoped to appeal to in order to carry it off.

'Night Bill,' Jared announced as he passed him, raising his hand and nodding in his usual friendly manner.

'Goodnight Mr Blake,' Bill replied looking up from the bank of displays.

Then, suddenly, Jared stopped in his tracks, cursing and muttering as though to accentuate his frustration.

'What's wrong Jared?' came Bill's concerned reaction.

'I've just realised I promised to do something for Van Tam and I forgot to do it…if he gets in before me in the morning and it's not on his desk, then he's going to rollock me…you know what he's like.'

'Well can't you stop here a little longer and get it done?'

'The thing is Bill, I need to get some photographs of the tech labs…he wants me to put together a presentation for some VIPs from South Korea next week who are keen to do a deal for a massive shipment of Dream units...Van Tam was going to give me access but I forgot all about it...and the last thing I want to do is disturb him at home.'

Jared looked at Bill and could tell he was trying to work out a way around his problem, and although not the most intelligent person on the staff list, he knew he didn't want to get into any more trouble with Van Tam, especially given his previous verbal warning. As Jared could detect he was about to receive some bad news, he elected to play his joker and waited for Bill's reaction.

'Is Meg still keen for me to teach her the piano? I know there's all kinds of new-fangled apps and holographic methods these days...but nothing beats the real thing, right?'

Bill had cottoned on to Jared's bartering technique and smiled, shaking his head at his deviousness.

'If anyone finds out about this...it wasn't me, right?' he exclaimed, now bringing up the list of staff on one of the displays and their corresponding access levels. 'I've given you Level-four access just for tonight...it'll return back to Level two after midnight so you better get whatever it is you need done before then.'

'That's great Bill...you're a star and don't let anybody tell you otherwise,' Jared replied and with that he made his way to the part of the building housing the lift down to the basement.

Jared knew where the doors to the restricted area at Dreamex were; he'd passed them on a countless number of occasions but had never been on the other side. That was until now and after placing his finger on the biometric reader and looking straight into the scanner's ocular recognition camera, he heard the door lock disengage and was quick to push it open and slide through. It appeared Bill's access update had worked.

As the door was fixed to tight springs, Jared watched as it arced back into place and automatically locked behind him. He now had to make his way to the lift down to the basement, just aft of the tech labs, where the assembly of the Dream Watcher took place and where the top secret science making up the machine's innards were protected. In fact, the technology was so advanced that Jared had heard Van Tam mentioning that they'd inserted a mechanism that acted as a self-destruct button; an inbuilt power source that would frazzle the internal circuitry and make it impossible for anyone to study if they tried to dismantle it.

After the door had closed, it was temporarily pitch black and Jared stepped forward tentatively, lights along the ceiling and floor of the long corridor automatically switching on after detecting his presence, like landing lights on a runway. There was nobody else about. He could see a couple of large rooms, to his left, glass fronted but with little visibility; shrouded in darkness; the only light being cast from the main corridor.

Pressing his face up against one of the Perspex screens, he could just work out what looked like a laboratory, although no equipment or components making up half-built Dream Watchers that he'd anticipated he might find. Instead, just rows upon rows of boxed machines, stacked high and wide; perhaps one thousand units right there in front of him, scope for a great many more given the room's dimensions.

Having been distracted briefly, Jared continued down the corridor, remembering his mission and retracing Van Tam's steps that he'd viewed via his Eye-Spy Lens feed a few days earlier. Taking a left turn just before reaching the end, he could see the lift doors and the keypad on the wall adjacent to it; clear signage confirming the restricted access. Jared walked up to the keypad, his hands a little sweaty by now and his heart beating a little quicker than before. He'd remembered the code that Van Tam had inputted, having been repeating it over and over again, but he still felt a great deal of jeopardy, anxious as to what might happen if he entered it incorrectly or if the code was a personal one allotted to Van Tam only. Would there be klaxons sounding and everyone alerted to a breach in security if it didn't work?

Wiping his hand on the sleeve of his U-neck sweater, Jared began typing in the eight-digit alpha-numeric code. He was confident he'd inputted it correctly; but nothing happened. The pause only acted to increase his stress levels. Then, suddenly, the lift doors began slowly opening. Jared blew his cheeks out in relief. He was in.

There were only two buttons on the lift panel inside and so Jared pressed the down arrow, its outline now illuminated and prompting the doors to close. Within a few seconds the lift came to a halt after reaching the basement. As the doors began to open, Jared was now faced with one of the most technically advanced set-ups he'd ever seen; hundreds of enormous floor to ceiling black towers, all flashing and whirring in unison. It was an impressive sight to behold. Jared had gained entry to the Super Computer.

Chapter 28

'I need to go back to headquarters, Tibbit. There's something I need to check on,' Van Tam exclaimed from the back of the car, the luxurious cabin offering him every conceivable option to help him relax on his hour-long commute.

'Of course Mr Van Tam,' came his chauffeur's response as he selected the appropriate exit off the shuttle-lane and readied himself to take over from the automatic pilot-mode.

***

Conscious that he didn't have time to stand there and admire it, Jared began examining the readouts at the ends of each of the towers and soon realised they were in both date and subject order. He just had to find Lorna's data. Making his way quickly along the rows, he then spotted it, the display on a tower towards the middle of the room; 'Lorna Matthews (2.6.37 – 21.3.42)'.

The dates were a reminder to Jared of her final dreams the night before her death. However, there was no time for any sentiment and he quickly took his bag from off his shoulder and placed it down on the ground, opening it up and carefully removing his Dream Watcher. He pressed the power button on the console and watched as the brain motif pulsed in blue neon to confirm it was active, before scanning the connections along the Super Computer panel corresponding to Lorna's dream data.

Given the amount of tech in the room, Jared realised that trying to connect his Dream Watcher to it remotely would be impractical, and so reached back inside his bag and pulled out a Dream Cable, attaching one of its ends into the socket in the middle of the brain motif and running it vertically up the side of the tower into a duplicate port. Jared then pressed the button next to it and there was an instantaneous reaction, his Dream Watcher now pulsing white. The small screen on the Super Computer tower confirmed a running total of the amount of data that had been successfully sent and it was only a matter of seconds before the figure had been replaced with the words 'DEVICE FULL – PLEASE REMOVE'.

Jared carefully prised the connector out from the tower and quickly placed his Dream Watcher back in his bag, before throwing it onto his shoulder again. After quickly checking that the screen had returned to its initial display and wasn't leaving any telltale signs to suggest he'd been there, Jared wiped down the buttons on the panel with a cloth from his pocket before making his way swiftly back to the lift.

***

'I won't be long...just need to pick up something from my office,' Van Tam confirmed as Tibbit stood by the open car door and waited for him to emerge.

Van Tam marched purposefully to the steps leading up to the entrance and made light work of them before making his way through the large glass doors. It was then that he noticed Jared coming from the direction of the restricted access area of the building; surprised to see him still there. Jared came over all hot and flustered at seeing his boss and did his best to conceal it.

'What are you still doing here? I thought you'd have left hours ago.'

'Just wanted to get something done before my time off,' Jared responded hoping his dedication to his job would placate him from any suspicion his boss might have.

'Are you sure everything's okay Jared...you seem a little on edge?'

'I'm absolutely fine Alex...just wanted to give myself an easier time next week on my return.'

'Well, I'm glad you're finally taking some time off...you need to relax and recharge...it's good for your brain too. Have you got anything planned?'

'Not much...just taking it easy and hopefully going to see an old friend,' Jared replied, realising how accurate his ad-lib response was, which made him feel more anxious.

'Do I know them?'

Jared didn't know if his boss was simply making chit-chat or if there was something more sinister behind his question.

'I don't think so, no. We went to school together...haven't seen them in ages.'

'Right, well I found out today that the ear-piece technology to complement the Eye-Spy lenses is almost ready, so plenty still to look forward to...have a good break and don't forget to capture your dreams whilst you're away.'

Jared nodded and smiled at Van Tam before continuing on his way towards the main entrance, resisting the temptation to look back across at his boss walking in the other direction towards the lifts up to the executive offices.

It was pitch black outside, the only light coming from the low-power solar lamps that dotted the now deserted car park. Jared noticed Van Tam's car in the drop-off bay at the bottom of the main entrance steps and kept his head down as he passed. Walking towards his car he could see Bill around one hundred yards away, his lit torch in hand as he carried out one of his routine patrols of the building's perimeter.

Getting into his car, Jared placed his bag on the front passenger seat and was relieved he'd made it out. He just hoped that he now had Lorna's data saved to his Dream Watcher.

Chapter 29

Although Jared knew he was away from Dreamex for a few days, he couldn't relax. He needed to check to see if he had successfully managed to download Lorna's dreams from the Super Computer. He'd spoken to Troy on his way home to relay what had happened and it seemed Troy was just as enthusiastic to find out; eagerly waiting at Jared's house and opening his friend's car door as he came to a stop on the driveway next to him.

'You managed it then?' Troy exclaimed, his face beaming as he patted his friend on the shoulder.

'Yeah, although had I been another couple of minutes down in the basement, Van Tam would have caught me...I bumped into him on my way out. I don't know whether he noticed I'd come from the restricted area but he didn't mention anything about that if he did.'

'Well, I guess we need to see if you have the data, right?'

'Yep, the Dream Watcher's in here,' Jared said passing Troy his bag. 'I need a drink, first,' he continued still feeling the tension mixed in with the relief of having seemingly got away with it.

After fixing themselves a drink in the kitchen and Jared having fed Sprocket and given him a fuss, they set themselves up in the cinema room. The pair realised that even if Jared had successfully captured Lorna's historic dreams, there would still be the painstaking job of searching through them meticulously in order to find one that would account for Lorna's mental health issues; the reason she'd lost her previous job, and why she'd ended up auditioning at Dreamex in the first place.

After connecting up his Dream Watcher to his other peripherals, it wasn't long until they received confirmation that Jared's covert operation had worked; the projection screen now displaying the contents of the Dream Watcher's inbuilt memory. They now had 2,016 individual files representing a portion of Lorna's back catalogue of dreams.

It seemed a little macabre and inappropriate, but with the task of scanning through each of them in turn, and both not having had much to eat that day; Jared had decanted out a large bag of sweet popcorn into a mixing bowl, which the two shared after selecting 'PLAY ALL' from the home menu.

After spending eight straight hours staring at the projection screen, they came up empty-handed; nothing they'd seen remotely suggesting it had anything to do with Lorna's previous problems. It was time to call it a night. They needed to sleep to ensure they were alert for when they continued the following day.

It felt very strange and a little sobering for Jared to be watching Lorna's dreams; serving as a reminder of how much he'd cared about her and selfishly hoping to see himself appear in one of them. But alas, he had not seen himself so far.

One thing Jared and Troy had been quick to agree on was to ignore any of the dreams that lasted less than five minutes; their logic telling them that if Lorna did have a recurring dream detailing the events that had caused her to go off the rails, then it was likely it would have been a more detailed and longer night episode. Having come up with the idea, they were buoyed to note that it had the effect of massively reducing the number of files they'd need to watch, although they were aware that the task was still an onerous one.

The pair continued to watch through the dreams the next day, just after lunchtime. They immediately discounted any that seemed spurious or conveyed happier times for Lorna.

Just as it seemed as though their idea had been futile and Jared's risks had all been in vain; they suddenly happened upon a more sinister dream and one that appeared dark from the outset. Both sat up, their attentiveness suddenly triggered.

The dream had started out by showing Lorna from her perspective. She appeared to be leaving a friend's house after dark, and after saying her farewells, the pair watched as she walked up to the front gate and out into a quiet and desolate suburban street, just the occasional street light offering her any visibility. There was a wooded area on the other side and the opening to a path through it.

Although realising that this was Lorna's dream, it still made Jared and Troy call out to advise Lorna not to take the path given it looked dangerous, especially for a woman on her own in the dead of night. However, it appeared the route back to Lorna's house was through the woods and with little hesitation; she slalomed her way through the barrier at its entrance and was soon heading that way.

They watched Lorna looking left and right at regular intervals; obvious that she was beginning to panic, her pace increasing and she began looking behind her. Jared reached for one of the cushions on the sofa and placed it on his lap, grabbing it with force as though to take out his pent-up anguish. Then, after she turned around once more, there it was; a shadowy figure hooded and dressed in dark clothing and seemingly much bigger than her. Whoever it was, they were following Lorna and it was evident that she was now looking forward, hoping to reach safety.

Jared moved the cushion nearer to his face, aware that the situation was desperate and there was nothing yet he could do about it. Turning round once more, Lorna was now looking straight at the person behind her, whose identity remained unclear.

Suddenly, Lorna began to run but seconds later she was forced back; the man having grabbed her. Despite trying to fend him off, Lorna was just not strong enough and was knocked to the ground. Jared closed his eyes, barely able to continue watching any more, Lorna's flailing arms trying to beat her assailant off and to protect herself. But she was unable to do it; the screen now displaying the bottom part of the man's face, who was smiling sadistically at her. The rest of his face was shrouded in darkness and the horrifying ordeal that it appeared Lorna must have experienced played out.

It was clear to both Jared and Troy that Lorna was recalling a horrific attack that she'd gone through and it wasn't difficult to see why she had suffered the nightmare as a result.

Jared pressed the pause button, not wishing to see any more of the terrifying encounter, especially as he knew that it must have actually happened to Lorna. Troy looked over at him.

'Well, we've found it', he exclaimed solemnly. Jared's response was two slow nods of his head, still gazing at the screen and obvious that he had been deeply affected.

After a brief pause, Jared spoke, turning to look at his friend.

'Let's do this…we've got to prevent him from attacking Lorna at all costs…if we spare her the physical and emotional damage of this ever happening, then we can hopefully save her.'

'Well I'm ready when you are,' Troy replied standing up and offering his friend his fist, which Jared met with his own in a show of solidarity and an eagerness to get the job done.

CHAPTER 30

'What if something happens to you, Jared? Say this attacker turns nasty and pulls a knife on you?'

'It's a risk I'm going to have to take, Troy...and besides; I've always got you as my escape route...hopefully just seeing me will cause him to think twice about attacking Lorna.'

'Why are you so desperate to save Lorna, anyway? You're not hoping she suddenly falls madly in love with you if you manage to save her, are you...saving the damsel in distress? What happens if you do manage it, and she doesn't? You might be setting yourself up for a monumental anticlimax which might have a profound effect on you.'

'With Lorna dying at Dreamex and because of the Dream Watcher, I feel partly responsible, even though I wasn't aware of the potential for the dream vortex...I realised she didn't have feelings for me years ago...I'd got over that...but you're right...maybe had this been one of the others I wouldn't even be contemplating it...I guess we all have that inbuilt compulsion to try to impress, or have those we are attracted to have cause to think about us; to reflect on what we've done or achieved...I didn't have to spend any time thinking about it...it just came naturally.'

'Right, well, you better get going then...let's get this done...just be careful...I can't come and help you, remember...once you're in there, you're on your own.'

After setting themselves up as before, Jared selected Lorna's dream from the on-screen menu once more, Troy's leg now manacled to the table leg by use of a more traditional and sturdy ligature; a thick six-foot piece of towing-rope.

'Remember, three taps and you can let go of me…and don't be pulling your arm out for any reason…scared the shit out of me last time.'

'Promise!'

With that, Jared pressed the play button and dropped the remote on the sofa before grabbing on to his friend, and as the image began to pan out, showing the sinister suburban setting, he began slowly climbing into the screen.

It was a wet and blustery environment that Jared found himself in, tapping out on Troy's arm and making a mental note of where his friend's arm penetrated the dream world. He was on a cobbled alleyway that ran along the back of a row of terraces, with very little visibility at all. A rat scurried across from a large communal recycling dumpster ahead and general detritus littered his path as he walked briskly to where he could see an opening up ahead.

Reaching the end, he came out onto a small crossroads and looking right could see a main road, a street light and trees lining the other side. Having witnessed the dream before, Jared realised immediately where he was in relation to the events that were about to unfold once again. He made his way swiftly across the road and found the entrance to the pathway that ran through the woods; the same one Lorna had taken.

Just as Jared appeared from between the houses, he looked right and could see a figure on the opposite side of the road. His gut feeling told him it was Lorna, but given the conditions and it was after dark, he was keen not to scare her; instead setting off down the path and away from her.

His plan was to forge ahead to the spot where the assault took place; to lie in wait to intercept Lorna's assailant before he had chance to attack her.

Having sped along the dimly lit tarmac path through the woods, Jared found some bushes and crouched down; his adrenaline pumping, ready to react and gearing himself up for a confrontation. His heart was racing now. However, the thought of someone attacking Lorna was enough to fill him with positive energy which he would use against the shadowy figure and do all he could to prevent it from taking place.

A couple of minutes passed and above the rustling of trees stirred up into a veritable frenzy by the strong wind, Jared heard the sound of footsteps coming towards him; the distinctive thudding of boot heels resonating against the hard surface, and getting louder and louder with every successive step. Jared was on high alert but ensured he could not be seen by Lorna as he lurked in the shadows.

Approaching Jared's position, Lorna turned around and it was evident that she'd heard something from behind her. Jared watched as Lorna then increased her pace and moved past him. He readied himself to pounce.

There was someone gaining on Lorna and they were now reaching Jared's position. It was time. Jared sprang out from the bushes and stood in the middle of the path to face them, the hooded character came to a halt a short distance from him. It was too dark for Jared to make out who it was. Lorna, having noticed what was happening behind her; stopped briefly, realising she was no longer on her own.

'What the hell do you think you're doing following a woman through the woods?' Jared hollered.

But no sooner had he finished his question than the person in front of him began slowly removing their hood. In the dim light Jared saw something that caused him to freeze; he could scarcely believe what he was looking at. He was looking at a carbon copy of himself.

Jared staggered backwards; the shock enough to throw him completely off kilter; temporarily forgetting the reason he was there. Lorna's attacker was Jared himself!

The confusion caused Jared to drop his guard, his doppelgänger seizing the opportunity and grabbed him by the scruff with one hand before punching him with the other. Blows rained in on Jared and he felt every single one of them as they made contact. He could feel pain in the dream world and with nobody to help him he knew he was in big trouble; Troy unable to see what was going on and helpless to act in any case.

CHAPTER 31

Trying desperately to fight back, Jared realised that his dream-double was not only much stronger than he but was now seeming to grow in size right before his eyes, making the task to defend himself much more difficult. His nemesis had now pinned him to the ground and was continuing his onslaught, Jared scrabbling around in the near pitch black for anything he could find to use as a weapon.

Fortunately, he laid his hand on a piece of wood, whilst trying to defend himself with his other as the assault continued. Jared swung the club at pace towards his assailant; striking his leg and forcing him backwards, making his double cry out in pain.

Before giving his attacker chance to retaliate, Jared was up on his feet and already running back to the alleyway. Despite his injuries, he ran quickly; his lack of fitness not slowing him as he knew his life depended on it. Almost tripping over on the cobbles and detritus of the snicket, he was overwhelmed to see his friend's outstretched arm and after tapping him three times was soon being pulled back into reality.

'What the fuck happened?' Troy exclaimed after Jared's face began emerging and noticing immediately he was in a great deal of distress.

'Just get me out of here!' Jared shouted in a desperate manner, pulling on Troy's arm, trying desperately to hasten his exit, hurrying through the screen and into his friend, sending them both falling backwards; Troy doing his best to help soften Jared's landing and the pair coming to rest on the floor next to the coffee table.

There was no conversation at all. Troy could hear his friend breathing hard and making involuntary noises, now sat with his back against the footstool, and looking tremendously relieved to be back. For Jared; things were even stranger. There were no signs of the injuries he'd sustained and the previous pain he had felt moments before had completely disappeared.

'What happened?'

As Jared managed to get his breathing back to normal, he looked up at his friend; Troy now having helped him up from the floor and onto the sofa, where he lay back and stared wide-eyed at him.

'That was crazy!'

'What was?'

'It was me Troy…'

'What the hell are you talking about?'

'The attacker…Lorna's attacker…in the dream…it was me!'

'I don't understand…how could it be you? You'd never do anything to hurt her…'

'It's a dream Troy…things don't always make sense in dreams…Lorna would have had the dream after meeting me and her subconscious placed me as her attacker… or the Dream Watcher interpreted her attacker as me…maybe there was a likeness and perhaps that's why Lorna was never interested in me given I looked a bit like him…except her interpretation of me in her dream was bigger and stronger than the real me...and hence able to beat the shit out of me...I was bleeding and he must have broken my jaw...but I can't feel any of that now.'

'Well if you were beating yourself up, then what about Lorna? Did she manage to get away? Perhaps you prevented her from being attacked and she's okay?'

'I hope so Troy...I really hope so...I'd need to take a gun with me if I had to do all that again.'

'But where would we get a gun from?'

Jared looked over at the pile of furniture and other bits in the corner of the room, before looking back at Troy.

'We can get hold of anything we want, remember...as long as I've dreamt about it...but there's something else I need to do also...'

'What's that?'

'I can't tell you, Troy...you're just going to have to trust me on this one.'

Chapter 32

'I've got something you might want to have a look at,' one of the Gatekeepers exclaimed in a serious tone after barging into Van Tam's office; little time for politeness and protocol.

'What is it?' Van Tam replied, having stopped what he was doing and stood up from his desk.

'It's Jared Blake's data...we uploaded his recent dreams that he handed in yesterday morning after coming back in after his break. When the data miners were scanning through them, I noticed something that seemed out of place.'

Van Tam appeared concerned given the abruptness and tone of the message and followed the Gatekeeper swiftly out of his office and up to the second floor, where the data miners were based.

Arriving at the bank of desks in question, the Gatekeeper unceremoniously swapped places with the data miner, and took over the controls of the holographic display, replaying the current dream that had been paused. It was one of Jared's most recent dreams and having found the part that had caused his dramatic reaction, Van Tam was now looking at it, turning his head away from the image briefly and rolling his eyes to the side, before looking back at it.

'So, he's managed to gain access to the Super Computer?'

'There can be no other explanation for it,' the Gatekeeper replied turning to look at his boss. 'There's no way he could dream about it in such detail otherwise...randomly imagining a Super Computer is one thing but his interpretation is a perfect likeness, as you can see for yourself.'

'He must have been down there last week…I saw him walking away from the restricted area when I came back to the office for something…he said he was working late as he wanted to finish something before he took time off.'

'But how did he obtain access?'

'I'm not concerned about that now…it's already happened. What I am concerned about is the reason why he was down there.'

After switching to the next Dreamers' data and setting it up on the display, the Gatekeeper stood up and beckoned to the data miner, who had walked away to another bank of desks.

'You can carry on with your work, now. We've seen what we needed to.'

Returning to Van Tam's office, both he and the Gatekeeper discussed the situation further.

'Well, ever since Lorna's death, Jared has not been himself…it's understandable after the event but it's been a few weeks now and he's still been acting strangely…can we pull up the corresponding security feed and get confirmation of his whereabouts within the building?'

The Gatekeeper brought up the security images from the evening in question and it wasn't long before they were witnessing Jared connecting up his Dream Watcher to one of the Super Computer terminals.

'What is he doing?' the Gatekeeper exclaimed looking at Van Tam with a confused look on his face.

'Well, that's obvious...it appears he's stealing dream data.'

Before the Gatekeeper could respond to his last statement, Van Tam asked him to leave, shepherding him out of the door and locking it behind him. He then walked over to a drinks cabinet cum bureau on the opposite side of his office, placing the index and middle finger of his right hand onto a biometric reader. The wooden facade slowly slid across to reveal a small hidden chamber with an elaborate throne at its centre, covered extensively with maroon leather, which had been designed to Van Tam's individual and precise specifications.

Moving into the small annex, the wooden facade automatically closed behind him and Van Tam took a seat, his arms and legs slotting perfectly into grooves in the leather padding and sitting back, his head now rested snugly inside a silver cube; only the front panel missing.

An aqueous screen then materialised in front of his face, forming the final plane and encasing Van Tam's head completely within. He was now looking at his Excellency, Santor Villamott CXXIV.

'Your Excellency,' Van Tam exclaimed, greeting his leader. 'What can you tell me about Jared Blake and the Super Computer? We have learnt that he has managed to infiltrate the room and appeared to be stealing dream data...but as yet we do not know of his intentions.'

'Alexander; Mr. Blake has discovered he can enter dreams. He has managed to obtain historic data for Lorna Matthews and is intent on trying to change her path within this reality in order to prevent her from having died at the hands of the

Dream Watcher. You must prevent him from doing so at all costs and before he compromises the entire project there on Earth.'

'Yes, your Excellency.'

'He has a friend; someone he has confided in and who is also aware of the secret. He is helping him to return from the dream worlds. You will need to deal with him also.'

'Your wish is my command, your Excellency.'

With that, the screen disintegrated enabling Van Tam to emerge from the cube and return to his office.

CHAPTER 33

The following evening just as dusk was turning to darkness; a horrendous lightning storm was in progress; heavy rain lashing against the ceiling windows of the cinema room in Jared's house and the noise deafening as a result.

Having obtained a gun from one of Jared's back catalogue of dreams, he and Troy were focused once again, Jared ready to re-enter Lorna's nightmare and try to stop his doppelgänger from attacking her. He knew he could not afford to let their appearance distract him again and would have to try to put it out of his mind.

'Those Eco-rods are going to be busy tonight,' Troy exclaimed trying to take their minds off the stress they were under, as they finished off the bottle of whisky in the kitchen.

'What happens if the lightning causes a power-out and the projector is fried whilst you're in the dream?' Troy asked, almost spitting out a mouthful of single malt as the idea suddenly dawned on him.

'We can't wait any longer, Troy…we need to do this now…the longer we leave it the more chance of someone realising what we're up to…I have a feeling Van Tam already knows something…I've tried to remain my usual self these past few weeks…but I can just sense it…the quicker we do this the better.'

The storm outside had caused Sprocket to feel a little jittery, his much more developed hearing causing him to bark incessantly with every clap of thunder. Leaving him in the kitchen on his own didn't help, but with much bigger things to worry about, they had no other option; not wanting to risk him jumping into Lorna's dream.

After the pair made their way up to the top floor, Jared placed the gun in his waist band underneath his pullover before helping Troy with the rope around his leg. It was time for Jared to relive the experience and after inserting the Dream Card that he'd saved Lorna's nightmare to; they could both see the familiar backdrop projected onto the wall. Jared took hold of his friend's hand once again.

'Be careful...and don't take any risks...dya hear me, Jared?'

'I promise,' and with that Jared blew out his cheeks as though preparing himself for battle, before disappearing from the room.

The first thing Jared noticed was that the injuries he'd sustained from his previous trip into Lorna's dream had returned and he felt the pain associated with them. His nose began dripping with blood and his jaw felt like it had been knocked out of shape. It was a shock to the system but he had to forge on through the major discomfort and as fast as he could.

Jared knew exactly where he was, and made haste for the woods again; this time seeing Lorna further off in the distance. He checked he still had the gun and was relieved to feel the handle protruding from his belt. Making his way along the tarmac path, he sought a better place to hide, pulling out the weapon and crouching down ready for a repeat of the confrontation. It was now just a waiting game again.

Troy was used to standing in the same position by now, with part of his arm inside the screen as he waited for his friend to return. He watched through the windows as the flashes of sheet lightning lit up the night sky as though it was daytime and counted the delay before the resulting thunder could be heard; and with it the simultaneous sound of Sprocket barking.

'Okay Sprocket! We'll be down soon,' Troy hollered to try to help comfort him. It seemed Troy's calls only served to accentuate Sprocket's barking as he could hear him getting even more spooked.

Lorna's footsteps neared and Jared knew he would soon need to confront his double once again. The thought freaked him out, but he felt more confident this time, increasing his grip on the gun, which he held down next to him.

Troy was suddenly surprised to hear Sprocket from the other side of the cinema room door and scratching the wood with his claws. 'How had he got out of the kitchen?' he thought. There was little he could do about it, having to remain with his arm inside the screen, and given Sprocket was still unable to enter; Troy had no choice but to listen to him barking loudly.

Having returned to a more relaxed state following his initial surprise at realising Sprocket had escaped from the kitchen; Troy was in for a much bigger shock. The door to the cinema room suddenly swung open and after Sprocket dashed into the room and straight up to him, a tall smartly dressed man wearing a full-length black woollen raincoat stepped through the doorway and stared piercingly at Troy.

CHAPTER 34

'Who the hell are you and how did you get in?' Troy shouted, the rain still peppering the ceiling windows and Sprocket continuing to bark.

'You mean Jared hasn't mentioned me before?' he replied as he slowly entered. Sprocket began to snarl at the stranger, Troy realising he was in a real predicament as he had to remain there in order for Jared to find his way back.

'My name is Alexander Van Tam,' he announced, with a menacing expression on his face, looking down at the dog that was now coming up close to him and barking. Van Tam crouched down and put his hand out towards Sprocket, now having calmed down and acting more inquisitive. In an instant, Van Tam grabbed hold of the dog's collar, picking him clean off the floor, and threw him headlong into the screen; a momentary yelp could be heard before the room fell silent, apart from the symphony of rain that continued to batter the windows.

'Why did you do that?' Troy shouted returning a more menacing stare.

'It was irritating me...and besides it was you I wanted to see,' the Dreamex CEO replied calmly and began moving towards Troy.

'Don't come any closer...dya hear me?'

Troy began stepping closer to the screen in a bid to stay as far away from him as he could, until he couldn't move any further. Van Tam took out an object from his coat pocket and with a nonchalant flick of his wrist Troy could see the six-inch blade, the projector beam reflecting off its shimmering surface.

'What the fuck are you doing?' Troy shouted, flinching backwards again, now terrified at the situation he found himself in.

Walking closer to him, Van Tam then crouched down and began slicing through the rope that was tied between Troy's leg and that of the table. Troy had a very bad feeling about it.

***

After Lorna had walked past Jared; he'd done his best to remain quiet and not alert her to his presence. He was now just waiting for his look-alike to appear. However, he couldn't see or hear anyone coming up the path behind Lorna.

Standing up, he peered around the bushes and tree foliage to get a better look. Suddenly, an arm thrust around his neck from behind and began choking him; taking him off guard. His instinctive reaction was to try to hit out with the frame of the gun, whilst also calling out; trying to alert someone to his predicament. To his shock; Lorna had doubled back on hearing his cry to see if she could help. She was the last person Jared wanted to see.

'Run!' Jared uttered as he managed to take a breath from the continuous choke grip that had rendered him powerless. It was his doppelgänger who had been hiding in the bushes waiting for Lorna. Instead of running away, Lorna picked up a small branch adjacent to the path and began beating Jared's assailant with it. The dim light and the shadows of the undergrowth had restricted visibility and she did not notice that the two fighting right in front of her were almost carbon copies of each other.

'He's after you!' Jared warned; his attempt forced and inaudible given the susurration of the rustling trees; his restricted breathing leaving him weak and unable to fight back any longer.

At that point there was a scampering of feet along the tarmac path and the barking from a small dog, racing up to Jared as he began losing consciousness; still with his doppelgänger strangling him. Sprocket began biting the ankles and lower leg of his master's enemy, snarling and baring his teeth. The dog received a kick, which caused it to squeal in pain and made Lorna even angrier.

Jared had finally let go of the gun following the mêlée, with just enough strength to kick it towards Lorna, who picked it up and stood pointing it at his attacker.

As Jared began slipping into unconsciousness, he could still hear the faint sound of Sprocket and of Lorna shouting at the attacker to let go of him.

As Lorna continued to hold the gun out, she was suddenly distracted by the sound of objects crashing to the ground nearby, followed by someone running up the path towards her from the other direction; someone who she'd assumed had heard the commotion and had also come to help. He was a black man, average build and with what looked like a small piece of rope tied around one of his ankles.

Turning her head for a split second, the attacker quickly thrust his arm out and tried to grab the weapon from Lorna. She was now in a life-threatening battle to keep hold of the gun.

Troy was getting nearer with every second and could see what was happening up ahead; but he didn't make it in time. There was an almighty bang, the noise relegating the other sounds into a quiet murmur. The gun had gone off and with it Lorna's struggle ceased immediately; she was now covered in blood.

Unable to regain enough breath following his ordeal, Jared's heart had come to a stop. Sprocket had been with him at the end, licking his face, as he slipped away; the sound of the gunshot the last thing he heard before losing his own battle.

***

Van Tam smiled as the dream finished playing on screen. He turned off the projector and removed the Dream Card from the peripheral at the back of the room and placed it inside his jacket pocket. Lifting the leg of the table, he then removed the length of tow-rope still attached to it, before leaving the room with it and back down the stairs and to the waiting car outside.

***

'He's stopped breathing! The readouts are off the chart…they're showing his glial cells have gone haywire,' one of the Dreamex scientists exclaimed as she monitored Jared's vitals on the screen in front of her in test-lab five.

'Wake him up! Wake him up! He's going into a dream vortex.'

Jared's heart rate had crashed and was now almost non-existent. The scientist patched through an emergency call to the on-site medics, but it was too late; Jared had flatlined.

CHAPTER 35

There was a deafening silence. The only things Jared could hear were the ad-lib script from his own conscience and the murmur of his beating heart; like a clock ticking the seconds away in a forgotten room; noticing the ophthalmic veins in his eyes pulsing in synchronicity. Jared lay there in complete serenity; a white haze shrouding him and the outline of a murky silhouette beyond; but he felt no pain any more.

His top lip felt cold as though wetted with blood from his nose; instinctively reaching a hand to it to discover the truth. At the same time, Jared sat upright and opened his eyes. Vibrant colours replaced the previous fog and with it a cacophony of noise whooshing in to fill his senses; almost too much to take in at once. It was a shock to his system; as though emerging from below the waterline of a swimming pool packed with boisterous children or turning on the television having forgotten it had been left on the loudest setting.

The silhouette now came into focus; an excitable dog approaching him on the bed where he lay, walking up his body on top of the duvet to lick his face. Jared put his hand up to prevent it from salivating over him again; opening his eyes wider. He realised he was awake, but his surroundings appeared very strange to him. It was the most surreal feeling he'd ever felt in his life.

It felt so surreal to Jared that he touched his arm to convince himself that he was real and actually part of the environment he had no recollections of; wondering where he was.

Jared was suddenly distracted as the bedroom door opened and a beautiful woman wearing a dressing gown entered, smiling at him and carrying two coffee mugs; a young boy of around ten years old having followed her in now diving on to the foot of the bed whilst clutching an action figure.

He recognised the woman immediately. It was the same woman he'd given a note to when catching the same bus home after work and who he'd fancied from afar. It still felt very surreal to Jared. For the moment, at least, he was still coming to terms with exiting a very vivid dream and waiting for his reality to calm the situation.

'You've woken up then? I've never known you to move so much during the night…were you having a bad dream?' she exclaimed, placing Jared's coffee on the side table next to him, before perching on the bed. Jared automatically moved towards the centre to afford her a little more room.

'When did we get a dog?' Jared asked, having pushed it sufficiently away from his face and patting its head, more through pretence than for any real desire to do so.

'Sprocket? You are joking aren't you hun? You told Charlie he could have one remember…about six months ago…you love that dog despite what you thought initially.'…

'Of course…I was joking,' Jared replied, now forcing a smile to convince her. 'Can I have a kiss, please?' he continued looking at her and realising she was more beautiful than he'd ever imagined.

'What's got into you today?' she replied bending over to kiss him, whilst ensuring not to spill her hot drink.

'Guess it must have been the dream I had...like the most bizarre one I've ever had.'

At that point Jared noticed a beautiful red dress hanging up from the wardrobe door at the side of the room.

'I hope your colleagues are complimentary about me wearing that tonight at your work's do,' she said, noticing Jared's prolonged gaze.

'You'll look amazing in it...'

'Well you've already seen me in it you dope...I tried it on for you last night, remember?'

'Sorry hun...just a bit tired...haven't woken up properly yet.'

'Well you need to get your hair cut today before we go...I know you said you hate getting it done but it looks a mess...I made you an appointment at the salon for later this afternoon.'

At that stage Jared noticed the action figure that Charlie was playing with, the young lad having been amusing himself with it whilst he'd been chatting with the girl from the bus. Stretching over towards him, Jared reached out his hand and took the figure from him, before lying back once again and scrutinising it closely.

'Where did you get this from, Charlie?'

'It was in one of the boxes you brought down from the loft full of your old stuff,' he replied. 'I was playing with it yesterday...you said it was called a Power Ranger.'

Jared held the action figure in front of him; predominantly red and white in colour and he suddenly had cause to reflect on his dream, trying to remember more about it. There were so many things that now seemed familiar and they were beginning to make more sense to him.

CHAPTER 36

'Can we watch Willy Wonka again later, dad...the original one?' Charlie asked politely and enthusiastically as he took the Power Ranger back off Jared.

Jared was left speechless at Charlie calling him dad. He had no recollection of him whatsoever and he was now even more confused.

'The old version, not the rubbish one with Johnny Depp in it,' Charlie continued realising his dad seemed distracted. Jared had a sudden flashback to his dream again, now hearing the music playing in his head, although unable to pinpoint its relevance.

'I only ever used to watch that at Christmas and just the once...you can have too much of a good thing you know,' Jared replied smiling at Charlie and pulled him towards him in a playful manner.

'Can we have scrambled egg inside crumpets again for breakfast, too?' Charlie asked full of enthusiasm for such an early hour of the morning. 'They tasted amazing.'

'That kid has an imagination just like his father...I don't know where he came up with that idea...well, you can have them if you like and perhaps watch the film with your dad later. I think you need to take that poster off your wall, first...what's wrong with having a poster of your favourite footballer, like your mates?' his mum exclaimed.

'What poster's this?' Jared interjected, not knowing what they were talking about.

'That poster of Cindy Crawford...the one you said you had on your wall at uni...Charlie found it in one of the other boxes you brought down from the loft and has been infatuated with it ever since, and he's now stuck it up on his wall above his bed...I wouldn't mind but it's a little too provocative and I don't think his friend's parents would be too happy if he has his friends over and they find out.'

'Your mum's right Charlie...you'll have to take it down...there's plenty of other things you can put up instead.'

At that point Charlie grimaced and ran out of the room, Sprocket chasing after him and down the stairs.

'Are you sure everything's okay Jared...you're acting very strange since you woke up?'

'I'm fine Lorna...just feeling a bit...'

'Who's Lorna?' she retorted in a very serious fashion; angry at Jared calling her by another name.

'Did I say Lorna? Sorry hun...like I said I had a very weird dream...'

'Who's Lorna?'

'I swear I don't know anyone called Lorna...I had a very vivid dream and there must have been someone in it called Lorna...'

'Well it's a shame I can't see what you were dreaming about...they need to invent a machine that can record them...my name's Anita, Jared...Anita! Please try to remember that...we've only been married 12 years.'

'Yes, I have a feeling they will do one day,' Jared replied under his breath, remembering something, as his wife marched out of the bedroom taking her coffee with her.

Jared felt guilty at upsetting Anita and yet fully aware that things did not seem normal at all. It appeared he was blessed with a beautiful wife and son but he had little or no recollection of them; questioning what was happening to him and what was wrong with his memory.

CHAPTER 37

Although still confused, Jared slid out of bed immediately and got dressed. He rummaged through the drawers of the bedroom furniture and spent time peering at the photos on the wall, noticing there were shots of him and Anita on their wedding day and of Charlie at different stages during his earlier years. He was still having difficulty remembering things about his life. With no alternative, he knew he had to carry on as normally as he could and hope that his memory would return, and with it the sense of belonging.

After walking out from the bedroom; Jared noted two sets of stairs; leading both up and down from the landing. His memory seemed to latch onto something now, remembering his old cinema room.

However, he realised his first task was to make up with Anita, so he descended the stairs down to the kitchen, where he found her. Jared was pleasantly surprised to learn she was a very forgiving person and one who obviously didn't do stubbornness at all; only a short delay after apologising before things seemed more amicable; although it appeared the reason for that was she had other things to discuss.

'I realise your head has been all over the place recently…what with the uncertainty over your job at the Bank…hopefully you'll find out what the changes are going to be soon and it won't be redundancies after all.'

Jared did remember he worked for a bank and that was something that hadn't altered since he woke. He enjoyed his job and got on well with most, if not all, of his colleagues.

As Anita gave Jared another hug she remained positive about their future together.

'And besides...if you are made redundant then they'll have to give you some sort of severance package, right? You've been there over thirteen years after all. You'll be able to do something you enjoy...you always said you were going to write a book one day...maybe it'll be your chance whilst you're looking for a new job...maybe it's fate and this was supposed to happen...I know you'll find something soon enough...something will come along that's perfect I know it and enable you to use that imagination of yours.'

'You're right hun...It may be the best thing that ever happened to us.'

'Oh and before I forget, we still need to look for a replacement for that table upstairs in the cinema room...what with Charlie putting a crack down one of its legs. I'm surprised you haven't been up there this morning, seeing as you only set it up a few days ago...don't tell me the novelty's worn off already?'

'Not at all...just wanted to spend time with you,' he replied, realising immediately how needy he sounded, although also aware that he may not have been completely out of the woods with her yet.

Jared walked through to the lounge and turned on the TV, switching the channel over to the news; wanting to remind himself what was going on in the world and hoping it would help trigger some more of his memories.

It was mid-way through a piece on SpaceX, stating that the company had failed in its attempt at creating a re-usable rocket propulsion system and that Elon Musk had given up on the idea of sending a manned mission to Mars. The following story centred on the new Contact-Tracing App that the government had rolled out in order to deal with future new spikes of COVID-19. The app had been received with great hostility in some corners, people suggesting that it was a ruse for the government to harvest personal data in order to keep tabs on everyone, as well as making billions from selling it on to large companies both in the UK and abroad.

As the programme went to a commercial break, Jared took the opportunity to make another coffee; but just as he was getting up, he noticed something which caused him to sit back down immediately. It was an advert for dog food. He couldn't recall having seen it before but the brand name seemed very familiar. As part of the ad, the CEO of the company was shown on screen and Jared was certain he'd seen him somewhere before.

'I'm Alexander Van Tam and I'm the CEO here at Dreamex, making the next generation of pet foods, providing your pet not only with the necessary nutrients and vitamins for a balanced diet, but now including an additional ingredient that will ensure your pet is free from worms and fleas without requiring any treatments or expensive trips to the vet...your pets will have sweet dreams with Dreamex.'...

Jared was certain he'd heard the name somewhere before and he recognised the CEO but couldn't place him. It was frustrating that he couldn't remember; another thing to add to a growing list of anomalies that somehow were connected to the dream he'd had, although now fading almost completely from his short-term memory.

Walking through to the kitchen and opening the cupboards, Jared found two large packets of Dreamex dog food; alerting Sprocket, who rushed in towards him expecting to be fed once again.

At that point, Anita entered, having spotted him, curious to see him crouched down and scanning a dog food packet so inquisitively. Noticing her, Jared placed it back quickly and stood up closing the cupboard door.

CHAPTER 38

A follow-up meeting had been called for in the crystal chamber of the Galactic Colonisation Research Programme in the Higher Sentient Galaxy. Its purpose; to discuss the changes put into effect following concerns raised over recent events taking place on Earth.

'What can you tell me about the project now...is it back on track?'

'Well, your Excellency; we have been successful in relapsing human evolution on Earth via a regression-warp as you instructed. Although still technically the year 2042, everyone will believe it is 2022; all development including technology has reverted back to where it was twenty years before. The majority won't have any recollection whatsoever and for those who we've been unable to eradicate all relative memory, then they will just convince themselves they're experiencing déjà vu...

Many will experience mild forms of 'holographic sickness' too, where they question their surroundings and their presence in what is their new reality. However, as we'd fine-tuned the process, then it went a lot smoother than the last time we carried one out on Ranhodfirsor. It's not perfect but it will certainly get the desired results.

'Will that cull the number of accidents? I seem to recall there were a great many on Ranhodfirsor following the shift.'

'Well, there will still be an increased number of acts of clumsiness as humans on Earth adjust to the regression-warp. A knock-on effect from transitioning will always catch out a few people, who may be prone to forgetfulness around their normal everyday lives. If these same people are in responsible jobs where amnesia is dangerous, then there could be a few serious accidents, yes…usually occurring in threes looking at previous data.'

'Let's see how they get on this time, shall we? And what about this Jared Blake character who discovered the portal into people's dreams?'

'We've fixed it so that his primary conscience is now present in a different world entirely to the one that he knew…we've ensured to surround him with plenty of telltale signs to convince him he'd been dreaming all along. We've also given him a wife and son as per his aspirations as a younger man; the woman he's married to is someone he thought about a great deal in his recent past, according to his hippocampus data…

That should at least make him happy when coming to terms with his new life. He's still working at the bank but even if he loses his job; there is no Dreamex for him to audition at this time. He may recall some aspects of what happened to him recently, but it'll be like a dream to him now; where everything seemed so vivid he can barely believe it wasn't real…but this will fade in time as he adapts and makes new memories…and has new dreams based on them…'

'Good, well, we need to be ready to reintegrate the Dream Watcher after another ten years have elapsed on Earth and hope that nobody works it out again…it's imperative for the whole project that it works…by my reckoning that should give us around six weeks relative to them before we need to push the button. Is there anything else we've done to try to improve the colony on Earth in the meantime?'

'Yes, we've transmitted a cerebral patch that will increase the human population's charitable persuasion. It will hopefully sway the majority to vote to help one another rather than cutting themselves off and looking to make money by any means necessary. There's no way of stopping the outcome, of course, and likely they'll still find a way, but we can monitor the situation.'

'Well, if that doesn't work and we still don't see better signs over the next 20 Earth-years, then we'll have no option but to eradicate them by way of an asteroid strike and ensure no survivors again.'

'Well what about the human colony on Ranhodfirsor? Looking at those figures, carbon dioxide, methane, nitrous oxide and ozone are less than one-third of that measured on Earth, although they're approximately 50 years behind regarding technological advancement. Maybe it's time to drop in the microchip and see how it plays out there.'

'Yes, it might be a good time to do that...I see greed doesn't appear to be as prevalent there yet. The two planets had exactly the same initial setup and raw materials as one another, don't forget. Happiness is at 62% over the population there compared to Earth's 37...perhaps technology is to blame.'

'Let's see how Earth evolves after the regression-warp has bedded-in. We can always start a new project on planets Galcus or Dasklan in the Celestial Quadrant using a different race entirely, if the humans continue to disappoint. We can set the time-lapse to 10-years-per-day to begin with so as to expedite initial colonisation. Eventually, we will be successful in finding the right balance and broaden our reach across the outer galaxies.'

CHAPTER 39

'Don't forget you said you'd help Charlie finish his school project too…he needs to hand it in on Wednesday, I think,' Anita exclaimed, now watching Jared systematically opening more cupboards in the kitchen before taking out a full bottle of single malt and staring at it.

'Project?'

'Come on Jared…what is wrong with you today? The project you've been helping him with about ideas for a greener future…in transport and energy…you came up with some great ones…Charlie loved the Eco-Rod.'

'Yes, of course…I remember; well I'll give him a hand this afternoon.'

'I think he'll just be playing on his Playstation all day if left to his own devices…you need to tell him a time and make sure he comes off it…I worry he isn't really interested in anything as far as a future career is concerned…at his age I already knew I wanted to be a lawyer…always remember my dad telling me I could be anything I wanted to be and he used to say 'never lose track of your dreams'.'

Jared almost dropped the whisky bottle as he instinctively turned his head towards Anita, with a pensive expression on his face. The last thing she'd said resonated with him greatly, although, again, he did not know why. He couldn't remember whether he was this forgetful normally or if it was still the after effects of his unconscious thoughts.

He was still suffering from bouts of amnesia and was desperate to find something or someone who could help him reinforce the foundations of his memory. He therefore decided to climb the stairs to his cinema room and after opening the door, noticed the retro arcade-machine in the corner under the sloping ceiling; remembering the old games that used to occupy his time; Space Invaders, Pac-Man, Frogger, Bomb Jack and his favourite, 1942. However, it felt like he hadn't played them in years.

Turning his attention to his projector, Jared slipped a Blu-ray disc into the player and switched on the system, taking a seat on one of the footstools nearest to the screen. He'd been drawn to Blade Runner and after the opening sequence had finished and the audience were introduced to Rick Deckard, the main character, he watched as the torrential rain lashed down on what had been a futuristic interpretation of Los Angeles 37 years after the film was first released.

For some reason, Jared suddenly found himself lured to the image on the wall. Getting up and walking towards it, he could see the picture quality was amazing and the rain seemed so life-like. Although it seemed a rather strange departure from reality, Jared held out his hand and moved it closer to the screen. Suddenly, he felt water on his hand and down his side. It was happening again.

Before the genuine shock could escalate any further, he suddenly noticed Charlie from behind one of the sofas, who, after having crept into the cinema room, was now stood up and continuing to spray his dad with his water pistol and laughing. Jared blew out his cheeks and closed his eyes for a second, before laughing himself, realising the situation and relief at the outcome.

'Come here you,' he hollered in a playful manner, and proceeded to chase Charlie back down the stairs. He caught up with him in the lounge, where Willy Wonka and the Chocolate Factory was already playing on the TV set.

It was at that point there was a loud knock at the front door. Jared stopped wrestling with Charlie on the sofa, and after smartening himself up and putting his serious face back on, walked out to the hallway to see who it was. Sprocket had begun barking as was customary for him on hearing the familiar sound and he now stood between Jared and the door.

'Okay, you...come out of the way,' he exclaimed, coaxing Sprocket back so that he could open it.

As Jared pulled the door towards him, he kept his foot in the gap to ensure Sprocket didn't get out or try to leap on whoever it was. Looking up, squinting slightly, as the sun shone brightly from behind them, it took a few seconds for him to work out who it was.

'It's me Jared; Lorna...it's great to see you again.'

CHAPTER 40

Lorna watched as his face lit up; a sincere expression that encapsulated both happiness and surprise in equal measure; as though seeing someone he thought he'd lost forever.

'It was all real Jared…you're not going mad…the Dream Watcher, Dreamex and saving my life…you're in one of your dreams right now…that's why you're with this woman and have a son…it's what you dreamt about after starting work at Dreamex…from your time working at the Bank. That's why you don't know your wife and son or have any recollection of them in your life…I'm here to save you and take you back to the real world.'

Although recognising her immediately; Jared remained speechless. He tried to recall why he did, her explanation triggering his memory and now some of it beginning to make sense.

'You remember Troy, right…your best friend?'

Jared smiled at hearing the name. 'Of course I remember Troy…we go back years…ever since playschool.'

'Well, Troy and I found this dream you're in now on the Dream Watcher you sent to my address. You wanted me to have it as you wrote down detailed instructions of what I needed to do in the event that you and Troy weren't at your house when I got there…your house in the real world. This dream you're in now is based on subconscious thoughts you had from your reality…do you remember?'

Realising what Lorna was saying sounded completely implausible, Jared stepped out from the house and closed the door behind him; conscious that he didn't want Anita to see the woman at the door. He definitely recognised Lorna and some of the things she was saying stirred his memory, but he was now becoming confused.

'Come on, let's go for a walk and get away from here...you can explain everything to me then,' Jared whispered, interested to learn more of what Lorna had to say, even though it was causing him a great deal of unease.

Finding a quiet park a couple of hundred yards away from the house, the pair sat on a bench overlooking an empty playground, and Lorna continued to describe the series of events that had played out.

'Troy told me everything about what happened...the fact that I'd died at Dreamex due to a dream vortex and that you hatched a plan to enter one of my dreams so as to prevent me from being attacked, although I have no recollection of that anymore. Your plan worked, Jared; that's why I'm here now to save you.'

'So where is Troy, now?'

'It's possible there's a version of Troy in this dream world...but the real Troy is back in your house in the real world and he's waiting to help bring us back. Do you remember anything about entering dreams through your projector screen?'

Jared looked pensive; realising his attempt at touching the rain during the Blade Runner film moments before must have been prompted by an earlier experience.

'Since waking up it's all felt very strange…like I really don't belong here…I don't remember anything about my wife and son, you're right…but there are some things that have made sense…things I've seen around me that I do remember…it all feels like a massive case of déjà vu. I put it down to the dream I'd had.'

'But it wasn't a dream Jared…it was all real…you died trying to save me from my attacker, a nightmare that I used to have regularly but which was becoming less frequent after I got the job at Dreamex. Troy told me that Van Tam forced him into my dream when he was waiting to help you get back…he couldn't fend him off as he knew if he did then you might be lost in my dream forever…

When Troy entered my dream, he made his way to where the attack had occurred along the path through the woods and saw me, you and my attacker. He said you were already dead; your face was covered in blood and you'd stopped breathing…my attacker had killed you. Troy tried desperately to resuscitate you but he couldn't bring you back.'

'So what happened to the attacker?'

'Well, you'd brought a gun with you into my dream because the first time you tried to prevent the attack on me, he'd overpowered you and beat you up. On that occasion you managed to escape back to the real world as Troy was waiting to pull you out. Seems the attacker caught you off guard hiding in the bushes the second time…he must have choked you as Troy said there was bruising around your throat. As he approached he could see the attacker grappling with me and then heard a loud gunshot and the attacker fell to the floor. When he reached me I had the gun in my hand…I'd shot him…using the gun you must have passed to me.

Because I'd killed my attacker, then he didn't rape me. You spared me from a terrible experience that would cause me mental health problems in the future. I didn't lose my job as a result and therefore didn't need to audition at Dreamex…I didn't die from the dream vortex, Jared…your plan worked.'

Lorna moved closer to Jared at that point and kissed him on the cheek with a great deal of affection and gratitude. Jared touched the part of his face where she had kissed him, still unsure about everything she'd described, but realised it sounded too complex for her to be making it up.

'So how is it possible you are here now to save me? You said Troy had been pushed into your dream…so surely that means he wasn't present in the real world…where you say you've come from.'

CHAPTER 41

'One day, a neighbour came to my door and handed me a package, saying she hadn't seen me for a while. It was from you and contained a Dream Watcher and a Dream Card onto which you'd copied my dream, the same dream you'd entered to save me; together with some instructions, details of your address and a key to your front door...

She also said that some official looking men had turned up at my home and gained entry, searching through the place, and probably looking for my Dream Watcher according to Troy...but she said you had given her strict instructions to only give the package to me in person and not leave it anywhere.

Your instructions to me stated that I should visit your house. If you or your friend Troy weren't there then things hadn't worked out as planned...and I should insert the Dream Card in the machine at the back of your cinema room and switch on the projector. You said I needed to put my arm into the screen if I saw someone that you described as your friend Troy.

I was able to pull Troy back into reality from my dream...but there was no sign of you...Troy said you had completely disappeared not long after you had died...he couldn't explain it but he said it was too dangerous to try entering the dream again to carry on searching for you...

He said it was a fantastic idea of yours to send a copy of my dream on another Dream Card to me, as Van Tam must have taken or destroyed the original one, because it was no longer in your cinema room...

With Troy back with me in the real world, he was able to explain everything that had happened, including how desperate you were to save me...

In the instructions you sent to me, you also mentioned your theory that if you had died whilst trying to save me, then you would no longer be present in my dreams. However; you said you would still be alive in yours and could still be brought back into reality from there. I know that sounds crazy...but they were your words, not mine...

Troy realised if we viewed another one of your dreams and saw you, then we could bring you back into reality. That was why you'd sent me the Dream Watcher with your dreams on. We connected it up and found this dream that you're in now...that's why I'm here...to help bring you back into the real world. We even brought your dog Sprocket back from my dream and I've been feeding him for the last couple of days...

Troy said Van Tam entered the cinema room when he was waiting for you with his arm in my dream, ready to pull you out. Van Tam threw Sprocket into my dream together with all the furniture and items that you'd brought back from other dreams...before overpowering Troy...

Troy saw all the items scattered inside my dream not far from where I shot the attacker...but I couldn't remember seeing them...like you're having difficulty remembering what I'm saying to you now...

He reckoned Van Tam was trying to get rid of all evidence that was linked to entering dreams...Troy was therefore surprised to see he'd left your projector and equipment intact and hadn't destroyed them too. Van Tam must have believed that with Troy and you trapped in my dream, there was no way any of us could ever make it back out into the real world, especially after he destroyed the original Dream Card.'

The more Lorna described, the more Jared was remembering his recent past, and she could tell he was beginning to believe her, despite looking puzzled.

'But hang on a second…some of what you've said I can get my head around, but…'

'Troy specifically said to tell you what you told him…when he questioned you about it…and that is 'not everything in dreams makes sense."

'Well, how do I know you are from the real world and not just part of this reality?'

'Troy is waiting to take us back right now…your memory will return once you're there. We really need you, Jared…we're in danger. You'll just have to trust me…the same way I must have trusted you, when you first entered your dream to try to save me…when I was dead and you couldn't bring me back despite your best efforts. Troy explained everything.'

'But what about Charlie and Anita…how do I know this isn't my real world and where I belong? If I leave them here, then won't it cause them a great deal of pain and grief?'

'The world around you here isn't real, Jared…as much as it all seems that way, Anita and Charlie haven't got any emotional attachment to you…in the same way you don't have for them…it's all make believe…your imagination being played out around you like characters acting out a script that you penned. Now come on, Dreamex has disappeared along with the Dream Watcher but Van Tam is still intent on eradicating us...we must be the only ones who know the secrets of entering dreams...'

Jared stared back at Lorna; trying desperately to recall parts of his memory that would help him abandon his doubts.

'Just give me a few minutes, please,' he said standing up from the bench. He began walking back towards the house, leaving Lorna sitting there, concerned at his sudden decision. 'I'll be back, I promise.'

Jared had always wanted a son but realised he would have to forfeit his utopian life. If Lorna was telling the truth, then he belonged in the real world; a world where it seemed he was very much needed.

Arriving at the house and entering quietly through the back, Jared could hear a familiar soundtrack emanating from the lounge.

Making his way there, he peered through the doorway, being careful not to be seen. Charlie was sat cross-legged on the floor in front of the TV, his eyes transfixed on the screen. He was watching his favourite film; the golden ticket winners and their guardians having entered the Chocolate Room of the factory, and Willy Wonka had begun to sing:

'...Come with me and you'll be
In a world of pure imagination
Take a look and you'll see
Into your imagination

We'll begin with a spin
Travelling in the world of my creation
What we'll see will defy explanation

The Dream Watcher

If you want to view paradise
Simply look around and view it
Anything you want to, do it
Want to change the world?
There's nothing to it

There is no life I know
To compare with pure imagination
Living there you'll be free
If you truly wish to be'...

ALSO AVAILABLE ON AMAZON

Printed in Great Britain
by Amazon